Fairy Tales from Grimm

OXFORD STORY COLLECTIONS

Fairy Tales from
Grimm

Translated by Peter Carter

Illustrated by Rosamund Fowler

OXFORD
UNIVERSITY PRESS

OXFORD
UNIVERSITY PRESS

Great Clarendon Street, Oxford OX2 6DP

Oxford University Press is a department of the University of Oxford.
It furthers the University's objective of excellence in research, scholarship,
and education by publishing worldwide in

Oxford New York

Auckland Bangkok Buenos Aires
Cape Town Chennai Dar es Salaam Delhi Hong Kong Istanbul
Karachi Kolkata Kuala Lumpur Madrid Melbourne Mexico City Mumbai
Nairobi São Paulo Shanghai Singapore Taipei Tokyo Toronto

Oxford is a registered trade mark of Oxford University Press
in the UK and in certain other countries

First published as *Grimm's Fairy Tales* 1982
Reprinted 1989, 1990, 1992 (twice)
First published in paperback 1997
First published in this paperback edition 1999

British Library Cataloguing in Publication Data available

Cover illustration by George Smith

ISBN 0 19 275011 9

3 5 7 9 10 8 6 4 2

Typeset by AFS Image Setters Ltd, Glasgow

Printed in Great Britain by
Cox & Wyman Ltd, Reading, Berkshire

Contents

The Golden Key

One bitter winter's day, when the snow lay deep on the ground, a poor lad went into the forest to gather sticks for the fire. The lad had thin boots and no scarf or gloves, and when he had gathered the wood he was so frozen with the cold that he made a fire to warm himself.

He scraped away some snow from the earth so that he could build the fire and under the snow he found a tiny golden key. Well, thought the lad, where there is a key there should be a lock, so he dug into the ground and found a chest made of iron.

The lad searched and searched but he could not find a keyhole. Then, at last, as the blue dusk crept upon him from the trees, he found it, although it was so small it was scarcely visible.

The lad blew upon his fingers and tried the key in the lock and it fitted exactly. Then he turned the key and, slowly, slowly, the lid of the chest swung open.

But now we must wait awhile until the lad has looked inside the chest. Then we shall see what treasures he found there.

1

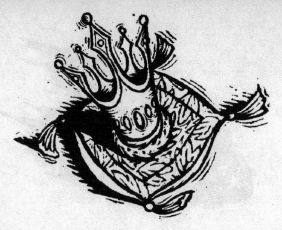

Rumpelstiltzskin

There was a miller once. His wife was dead but he had a daughter called Anna who was clever.

The miller was a little red-faced man who was always boasting about how clever his daughter was. In fact he boasted about her so much that when his neighbours saw him coming they used to hide.

One day the King of the country came riding through the town. The miller could not bear that the King should ride away without hearing how clever Anna was so he actually ran from the crowd and grabbed hold of the bridle of the King's horse.

'Your Majesty,' he cried, 'I have a daughter who is very clever.'

The King looked down on the miller. 'Well,' he said, 'I am glad to hear it.' Then he gave his horse a touch of the spur and rode on. But the miller ran after him and seized his stirrup.

'You don't know how clever my daughter is,' he shouted. 'She can do anything. She can read and write and do arithmetic and play the piano and she can sew and weave and cook . . . '

2

What an idiot, thought the King. 'Good,' he said. 'Good,' and he winked at the crowd and rode on.

The crowd burst out laughing and the miller was so vain that he could not stand it.

'Your Majesty,' he called, 'you don't understand. Listen, my daughter is so clever that she can spin straw into gold!'

'What?' The King reined in his horse and stared at the miller. 'What did you say?'

The miller could have bitten his tongue off but he could not go back on his word with all the people watching him.

'That's right,' he said, 'she can spin straw into gold.'

The King could not believe his ears but he liked gold as much as the next man so he told the miller to bring the girl to his palace that very day.

When Anna got to the palace the King took her to a small room.

'Now,' he said, 'here is a bale of straw and a spinning-wheel. I will come tomorrow morning, and if you have not spun the straw into gold then you will die. No one is going to make a fool out of me. Now get on with it.'

Then he locked the door and left Anna alone.

Anna sat by the spinning-wheel and began to cry. 'If I was locked in this room for the rest of my life,' she said, 'I could not spin one wisp of straw into gold.'

But as Anna sat weeping a little door opened in the wall and a dwarf jumped into the room! Anna screamed when she saw the dwarf, who was as ugly as sin, but the dwarf put his fingers to his lips.

'Now, now,' he said. 'There's no need to scream. I'm not going to eat you. No, no. But I heard what the King

3

said. Now, what will you give me if I spin the straw into gold?'

Anna was wearing a necklace and she gave it to the dwarf. 'You can have this,' she said. 'It belonged to my dear mother.'

The dwarf had a good look at the necklace. 'Very well,' he said. 'That will do.' And he sat at the spinning-wheel and spun the straw into gold. Then he left through the little door.

The next morning the King came with his executioner, because he meant what he had said, but when he saw that the straw had been turned into shining gold he was very pleased and he sent the executioner away.

The King was pleased, but at the sight of the gold he became greedy. 'I will make this miller's daughter spin more gold,' he said, and that night he locked Anna in a bigger room with *three* bales of straw.

'Now,' he said, 'spin this into gold or I will have you killed. I mean it.' Then he locked the door and went off to a party.

Again Anna sat and wept, and again a little door opened and the dwarf came out and said that he would spin the straw into gold.

'But what will you give me?' he asked.

Anna took off her ring. 'I will give you this,' she said. 'It was my dear mother's.'

The dwarf looked at the ring, bit it to make sure that it was real silver, said that it would do, then sat down and spun the straw into gold. When he had finished he went through the little door and left Anna alone.

In the morning the King came, and when he saw the gold, greed seized his heart and he took Anna into a huge room with enough straw in it to thatch every house in the world.

'Spin this straw into gold,' he said, 'or you know what will happen to you.' Then he left.

Anna wept and cried, but a little door opened and the dwarf came out and said that he would spin the straw into gold.

'But what will you give me?' he asked.

Anna shook her head and cried. 'I have nothing left to give you,' she said.

The dwarf rubbed his chin. 'Hmm,' he said. 'Well, I'm certainly not going to work for nothing. Still, I'll tell you what I will do. If ever you become a queen then you must give me your first-born child.'

'Give you my child?' Anna said. 'How could I do such a thing?'

The dwarf shrugged. 'All right,' he said. 'It's all the same to me. You stay here and tomorrow the King will have your head chopped off.'

He went to his little door but as he was going through it, Anna thought, I am only a poor miller's daughter. How can I ever become a queen? and so she said, 'Wait, I agree.'

The dwarf turned around and rubbed his hands together. 'Good,' he said. 'That's a promise,' and he spun all the straw into gold and then left.

The next morning the King came and saw the gold. 'Excellent,' he said. 'This is wonderful. Now I have all the gold that I shall ever need. Anna, you need never spin straw into gold again.' And he was so delighted that he took Anna off to the cathedral and married her.

The summer came and the summer went, and the autumn and the winter came and went, and then, in the spring, Anna had a baby daughter. How she loved the child! She loved it so much that she could not bear to spend one moment away from it; and she was so happy that she quite forgot about the dwarf who had spun the straw into gold; and she quite forgot, too, the promise she had made to him.

But the dwarf had not forgotten. No. And one day, when the King was at the dentist having a tooth pulled out, a little door opened in the nursery wall and out came the dwarf!

He saw the baby in its cradle and he scampered to it and tickled its toes so that the baby laughed and gurgled, for the child had not yet been taught to see ugliness.

'Ah,' said the dwarf. 'What a bonny baby. Yes, and it is mine!'

When the Queen heard that she almost fainted, but the dwarf stamped on the floor.

'You promised,' he shouted. 'You promised me your first-born child if you ever became queen and now I have come for it.'

The Queen wept and wailed and went down on her knees before the dwarf. She said that she had never dreamed that she would become a queen, and she said that she would give the dwarf anything in the kingdom if he would only leave her the baby.

But the dwarf would not listen. 'No,' he said. 'I want the baby. You must keep your promise.'

The Queen said that if the dwarf took her baby she would be heart-broken and lonely, but the dwarf shook his head.

'What about me?' he said. 'I am lonely, too, and no woman will ever marry me so that I shall never have a child of my own unless I take this.' And he tickled the baby's toes again.

Ah, how the Queen wept. She held the baby in her

arms and cried so much that the baby was sopping wet. She cried so much that in the end the dwarf could stand it no longer.

'All right,' he said. 'All right, all right. I'll tell you what I will do. I will give you another chance. I will come here at midnight for the next three nights and if you can guess my name then you may keep the baby.' Then he left through the little door.

The Queen sat rocking her baby for a while and then she sent for her huntsmen and foresters.

'Listen,' she said. 'Somewhere in the world there is a dwarf. I do not know where he lives but you must find him and discover his name. And you must do this within three days.'

The huntsmen and foresters thought that was a tall order, but they loved the Queen so much that they were ready to obey and so they mounted their horses and rode off to the four corners of the earth.

All day the Queen sat at her desk writing down all the names she could think of. Then, that night, as the great palace clock struck twelve the little door opened, and the dwarf came out and asked the Queen if she knew his name.

'Is it Matthew?' asked the Queen.

'No!' said the dwarf.

'Is it Mark?'

'No!'

'Is it Luke?'

'No!'

'Is it John?'

'No!'

And the dwarf laughed, tickled the baby, and ran through his little door.

All the next day the Queen waited for the huntsmen and foresters but none returned. At midnight the dwarf came again and asked the Queen if she knew his name.

This time the Queen tried all the funny names she could think of.

'Is it Knobbly-knees?'

'No!'

'Is it Baldy-head?'

'No!'

'Is it Cross-eyes?'

'No!'

'Is it Blue-nose?'

'No, no, no!' cried the dwarf, and he laughed, tickled the baby, and ran through his little door.

The Queen lay awake all that night trying to think of names and hoping that the foresters and huntsmen would come with the dwarf's name. But during the day the servants came riding in one by one and they all said that they could not find the dwarf, nor find out his name.

Up and down the palace walked the Queen, hugging her baby, and crying because she knew that she would never guess the dwarf's name, and so she would lose her baby forever.

The night came and the Queen thought she would die of grief, and then, at five to twelve, she heard a horse gallop through the palace gates, and the last huntsman dashed into the nursery, panting and covered with dust.

'Ah, your Majesty,' he cried. 'For three days I have been searching for the dwarf and, last night, when I was in the wild forest, I saw a spark of light. I rode towards it and saw a little house with a fire burning outside it—and dancing round the fire was a dwarf!'

The huntsman wiped his face and had a glass of wine. 'Yes,' he said, 'the dwarf was dancing round the fire and he was singing a song. I crept through the bushes as if I was stalking a wolf and I heard the song the dwarf was singing. This is it:

"Today I brew, today I bake,
Tomorrow I will the baby take.
For the Queen will lose the game,
RUMPELSTILTZSKIN is my name!" '

When the Queen heard that she danced for joy. And then the great clock began to strike twelve, the little door opened, and the dwarf came in.

'Well, Queen,' he cackled. 'This is your last chance. Tonight I will have the baby. See what I have brought—' and he showed the Queen a nightgown, a rattle, and a dummy.

But the Queen raised her finger. 'Wait,' she said. 'First I have a chance to guess your name.'

The dwarf laughed and clapped his hands together. 'Guess away,' he said. 'But you will never guess it in a million years.'

'That may be,' answered the Queen, 'but I am going to try. Is it Martin?'

'No!' cried the dwarf.

'Is it Conrad?'

'No!'

'Is it Heinrich?'

'No! No! No! No! No!' The dwarf jumped up and down, squeaking with pleasure.

'Well,' said the Queen, looking sad, 'I have one guess left.'

'Yes,' the dwarf nodded. 'One guess and only one, and you had better get on with it because the clock is striking twelve.'

The Queen leaned forward. 'I can hear it,' she said. 'Now, let me think. Is your name . . . could it be . . . might it possibly be . . .' And as the great clock struck the last chime of midnight, she shouted, 'RUMPELSTILTZSKIN.'

'Yahee!' The dwarf screamed and his face was red with rage. 'The Devil told you that!' He stamped the floor so hard that his leg went right through it. It went in so far that he could not get it out so he took hold of it and pulled so hard it came clean off. Then he stamped again and went through the floor and he has never been heard of, nor seen, since that night.

And so the Queen kept her baby and was very happy with it. But still, you know, it was sad for the dwarf who wanted to have a child of his own to love and care for.

The Cat and the Mouse

In the days when wishes always came true, and that was some time ago, a cat and a mouse lived in a church. One day the cat went to the mouse-hole and called down it.

'Miss Mouse,' it said, 'why don't we set up house together? We could live in the belfry and, as they say, two can live as cheaply as one.'

The mouse stroked her whiskers and peered through the hole, but the cat had such a nice smile and purred in such a friendly way that the mouse thought, Why not? After all, it was true that two could live as cheaply as one and the mouse was hard up, anyway.

'All right, cat,' she squeaked. 'It's worth a try.'

'Good,' said the cat. 'But just let me say this. Soon it will be winter and it will be hard to find food so we ought to buy some now and store it. What do you think?'

The mouse thought it was a good idea so they put their savings together and bought a blue jug full of cream.

'Now,' said the cat, 'we ought to put this cream where nobody can find it. You know what some people are like,

11

they would steal it even if it is in a church. Where do you think we should hide it?'

The mouse thought and thought but she could not think of anywhere safe. 'I give up,' she said. 'What do you think?'

The cat scratched her ear for a minute or two and then her eyes lit up. 'I know,' she said, 'we will put it under the altar. Nobody goes under there and the altar cloth will hide it.'

The mouse agreed and so they hid the cream underneath the altar.

'But we must not touch it,' the mouse said. 'We must save it for the bitter days of winter.'

'Of course,' said the cat and looked quite offended. '*I* won't touch it, that's for sure.'

A week or so went by and the cat and the mouse lived happily together in the belfry. But after a while the cat began to lust after the cream. All day long she thought about it and all night long she dreamed about it. In the end she could stand it no longer and she thought of a plan which would let her get to the cream. One morning she went to the mouse.

'Miss Mouse,' she purred, 'I want to tell you something. My cousin was married last year and now his wife has had a kitten. It is a beautiful kitten, snow white with brown flecks. My cousin wants me to be the god-cat and hold the kitten over the font when it is baptized. Will you mind if I go?'

'Of course not,' the mouse said. 'I will get on with the housework. Give my best wishes to the kitten, have a good time, and when you drink the good red Christening wine think of me and bring some back. I should like a drop.'

'Certainly,' said the cat. 'And I will bring you some Christening cake as well.'

She licked her lips and left the belfry but she was not going to a Christening at all! Instead she went straight to the altar, crept underneath the altar cloth, and licked the top off the cream. Then she went for a stroll on the roof tops of the town.

In the evening she went back to the church, ran up the steps of the belfry and sat down by the mouse.

'Did you have a nice time?' the mouse asked.

'Oh yes, very nice,' said the cat.

'And did you bring me some wine and cake?'

'Ah,' the cat said, 'I'm very sorry, I did get you some but a big dog chased me and stole them.'

'They ought to do something about those dogs,' the mouse said. 'Still, never mind. What did your cousin call the kitten?'

The cat thought of the cream and smiled. 'Topoff,' she said.

'Topoff?' cried the mouse. 'That's a funny name.'

The cat stopped smiling. 'What do you mean, funny?'

'Oh . . . er . . . nothing,' answered the mouse. 'Nothing at all. It's just that I have never heard the name before. Sorry.'

A few more days passed and the cat began to long for the cream again. Night and day she thought of the great blue jug and the thick, yellow cream standing under the altar. At last she went into the kitchen where the mouse was washing the dishes.

'Miss Mouse,' she said. 'Another cousin of mine has had a kitten. It is a beautiful creature, black with a white ring around its neck. I have been asked to be the god-cat and hold it over the font when it is baptized. Do you mind if I go?'

13

'No,' said the mouse. 'Go by all means. But bring me back some wine and cake, please.'

The cat said that she would and ran from the belfry and went straight to the altar. She crawled under the altar cloth and licked up half the cream! Then she slept on the roof of the mayor's house until evening, when she went home.

'Hello,' said the mouse when the cat pattered into the belfry. 'Did you have a nice day?'

'Ah, yes,' said the cat. 'It was a very nice day,' and she smiled blissfully.

'And did you bring me some wine and cake?' asked the mouse.

'I did,' the cat said, 'but that big dog I told you about, the one that chased me last time, it ran after me again and stole the wine and cake.'

'I'm sorry about that,' said the mouse, and she was, too. 'Still, what's done can't be undone. What did they call the kitten?'

The cat closed her eyes and thought of the cream. 'Halfempty,' she said.

'Halfempty?' squeaked the mouse. 'What are you saying? I've never heard of a name like that in all my life!'

The cat opened her eyes and the smile vanished. 'Well, what of it?' she said. 'You don't know every name in the world, do you?'

'No . . . no . . .' said the mouse. 'It's just that it seems strange, that's all.'

Another week passed and again the cat began to dream of the blue jug and the cream. Cream! she thought, Cream! I must have it. I must, I must, I must. And I will!

The next morning she went to the mouse and said, 'Miss Mouse, another cousin of mine has had a kitten and she wants me to be the god-cat and hold it over the font when it is baptized.'

'Another god-kitten?' said the mouse.

'Yes.' The cat licked its lips. 'But this is a very special kitten. It is black with white paws but there is not another white hair on its body. A kitten like that is born only once every seven years and it is a great honour to be asked to be its god-cat. May I go?'

'Mmm,' said the mouse. 'You certainly have plenty of god-kittens; first Topoff, then Halfempty, now this. Still, I suppose if you must go then you must.'

'Thank you,' said the cat. 'And I will bring you some wine and cake.'

The mouse stayed in the belfry and made everything neat and tidy while the cat slid underneath the altar cloth and licked up the last of the cream. Then she climbed up an apple tree and dozed the afternoon away.

At six o'clock the cat went back to the belfry and the mouse asked her if she had enjoyed the baptism.

'Oh yes,' said the cat. 'All the family were there and I held the kitten over the font. It is a beautiful kitten, really beautiful. Oh, and I'm very sorry, I had some wine and cake but—'

'Don't tell me,' said the mouse. 'That big dog chased you again and stole them. Anyway, what did they call the kitten?'

The cat's eyes turned into green slits and it showed the tip of its tongue as it thought of the cream. 'They called it Allgone.'

'Allgone?' cried the mouse. 'Allgone? Eeh, eeh, eeh! That is the most amazing name I have ever heard of.

Allgone! What can it possibly mean? I have never seen it in the newspapers or the Bible, and it isn't in the Calendar, that's for sure.'

'It is an old family name,' said the cat. 'Anyway, what has it got to do with you what we call our kittens? It's a free country, isn't it?' and just for a moment she showed her claws.

The mouse looked at the claws then shook her head. 'All right,' she said. 'All right. It's your affair.' Then she curled up in a scrap of wool and went to sleep.

The summer ended and the autumn came and went, but the cat was not asked to be a god-cat again. Then the winter came and the snow fell and covered the town and there was no food to be found anywhere. One morning the mouse went to the pantry and looked into it. She shook her head and went into the sitting-room where the cat was dozing.

'Cat,' she said. 'There is no food left in the house. Thank goodness we had the sense to store the cream underneath the altar. Let us go and have some now. I shall enjoy that.'

I'll bet you will, thought the cat, and she trotted to the altar with the mouse scurrying behind her. The mouse put its paw on the jug.

'Now for it,' she said, climbed up the handle, peered inside, and almost fainted!

'Aiee!' she squeaked. 'Aiee! Now I understand.' She looked at the cat and her whiskers quivered with anger. 'When you said that you were going to the baptisms you were coming here and stealing the cream. Yes, I see it all, now, it is as clear as daylight. First, Topoff, then Halfempty, then—'

'Watch it!' yowled the cat. 'One more word from you and I'll . . .'

But it was too late. The word was already on the poor mouse's tongue. 'Allgone!' she squeaked and she had hardly got the word out of her mouth when the wicked cat sprang on her and swallowed her right down before you could say Jack Robinson.

Sweet Rampion

I n a land beyond the seas, there was a man and his wife who longed to have a child of their own. Many years passed but no child was given to them until there came a time when the woman knew that God was going to grant her deepest wish.

From their window the man and his wife could see into a magnificent garden, full of flowers and herbs. The garden was enclosed by a wall although that was unnecessary because, in any case, no one dared to enter it for it belonged to a witch who had such strange powers that she was feared by the entire Kingdom.

One day the woman was sitting in her window and she saw that growing in the herb bed was a mass of rampion. The rampion was so fresh and green that the woman longed to eat some in a salad. Every day she looked down on the rampion, and every day her desire for it increased. But, as she knew that the witch would never let her have any of the rampion, she grew pale and ill.

Her husband noticed how thin and sick his wife's face had become. One night, when he got home from work,

18

he held her hand and said that he was going to get the doctor.

His wife shook her head. 'No,' she murmured. 'A doctor cannot help me.'

'But what is the matter?' asked her husband. 'You must tell me. If I don't know what is wrong with you then I can't help you, and if I can't help you then I shall be ill myself.'

'Ah,' said the wife. 'It is the rampion in the witch's garden. If I do not get any to eat then I shall die.'

Well, thought the man, sooner than that any harm should come to my wife I will climb into the garden and steal some rampion. Yes, even if it costs me my own life.

That night, at dusk, the man climbed over the wall into the witch's garden and took some rampion. He gave it to his wife who made a salad and ate it, and at once a little colour came back into her cheeks. She felt so much better that she longed for more rampion, but she did not tell her husband because she did not want him to risk his life again for her.

But the husband was no fool. He saw how the colour was fading again from his wife's cheeks and so, after a few days, he crept into the forbidden garden again and gathered an armful of rampion. Once again his wife made a salad, ate it, and was better. But again she sickened and so, for the third time, the man climbed into the garden and he took a basketful of rampion. But as he looked up he almost died of fright for there, standing over him, was the witch.

'Ah,' said the witch, and her voice was as sharp and as cold as the north wind. 'Ah, how dare you creep into my garden and steal my sweet rampion. You will suffer for this.'

The man fell on his knees and begged forgiveness.

'Show compassion,' he cried. 'The rampion is for my wife. She is going to have a baby and if she does not have the rampion then she will die.'

In the moonlight the witch's face was cold and white and terrifying, for, although she was not ugly, yet she seemed full of ugliness, and although she did not look evil, yet evil seeped from her like poison gas. But at last she nodded.

'Very well,' she said. 'Take all the rampion you wish. But as you have taken from me, so shall I take from you. When your child is born I will come and have it for my own.'

What could the man do? He was powerless before the witch and so he took the rampion and walked sadly away.

However, the woman grew healthy on the rampion and, in time, she had a baby daughter. But before it was a day old the witch appeared and took the child away.

The witch called the child Sweet Rampion and it grew into the most beautiful girl under the sun. But the witch could not bear that anyone else should see the child's beauty and so, when Sweet Rampion was twelve the witch took her into the forest and locked her in a room high in a tower of grey flint which had neither a door nor stairs but only one small window, forty feet high. When the witch wanted to visit Rampion she stood at the foot of the tower and cried:

> 'Sweet Rampion, Sweet Rampion,
> Let down your hair to me.'

Rampion had wonderful hair, as fine and as strong as gold thread, which she wore in braids. When she heard the witch call she unbraided her hair, wound it once around a hook over the window, and let it fall to the ground. Then the witch would climb up it.

Six years passed and Rampion grew from a girl into a woman. All the livelong day she sat in her tower, embroidering, playing on the harp, and singing. One day it happened that the King's son came riding through the forest. As he passed the tower he heard Rampion's song and it was so pure and sweet that he was enchanted. He rode around the tower looking for a door but as there was none he had to ride home, sadly disappointed. But the singing had so enchanted him that every day he was drawn back into the forest, as if by a spell, and listened to the pure, sweet voice drifting from the bleak, impregnable tower.

But still he could not find a way in and he despaired of ever seeing the sweet singer until one day, as he stood hidden in the trees, the witch came and sang:

> 'Sweet Rampion, Sweet Rampion,
> Let down your hair to me.'

Rampion let down her golden tresses and the witch climbed up. 'So,' said the Prince, 'that is the ladder. Well, I shall try my luck that way, too.'

The next day the Prince went to the tower and waited until the first bats flitted through the trees. Then he stood under the window and called:

> 'Sweet Rampion, Sweet Rampion
> Let down your hair to me.'

Rampion heard the call and let down her hair and the Prince climbed up.

When he appeared at the window Rampion was shocked and frightened, for she had never seen a man before or, indeed, anyone but the witch. Still, the Prince was gentle and spoke so softly, that she lost her fear, and when the Prince asked her to take his ring as a token of love she laid her hand in his and took it, For, she thought, he will surely love me more than the witch does.

'I would go with you this very night,' she said. 'But how could I get down? What you must do is this. Each time you come bring a skein of silk. I will weave a ladder from the silk and when it is finished I will climb down it and ride away with you.'

The Prince agreed, and every evening he came to the tower with a skein of silk; and every day Rampion worked, weaving the ladder for her escape.

Now the witch knew nothing of this until one day, when she had climbed up the tower, Rampion said, innocently, 'Why do you take so long climbing up my tresses? The young Prince climbs up in a second.'

The witch stared at Rampion. 'What did you say?' she asked.

Rampion smiled nervously. 'Only that the Prince climbs quicker,' she said.

'Aah!' The witch raised her hands and her fingernails were like the dry claws of a vulture. 'What is this you say? Aah! I thought that I had hidden you from all the world and yet you have deceived me. Aah!' Again she raised her hands and now they looked yellow and wrinkled, like the claws of a chicken. She struck at Rampion and seized her by the hair.

'Now!' she spat, 'Now!'

She twisted Rampion's hair in her left hand and with

her right hand she took a pair of scissors. Slash, slash, slash! Off came Rampion's golden hair. The witch laughed. 'No man will ever climb up to you again,' she shrieked. And then, so pitiless was she that she took Rampion into a desert and cast her off so that the girl had to live among the wild beasts.

When the witch had finished with Rampion she went back to the tower and climbed up Rampion's hair which she had tied to the hook over the window. Then she waited, crouching by the window like a cat before a mouse-hole.

At evening the Prince came and stood at the foot of the tower and sang:

'Sweet Rampion, Sweet Rampion,
Let down your hair to me.'

The witch smiled an evil smile and threw down Rampion's hair. The Prince climbed up; but instead of his true love he found the witch waiting for him, and she looked a thousand years old.

The witch laughed and folded her arms and rocked to and fro. 'Ha ha,' she crowed. 'Ha ha. You have come for Rampion but that bird is no longer singing in the nest. No, the cat has got it, and now the cat will scratch your eyes out for you.'

The Prince was sick with grief. So great was his despair that he threw himself from the window. But as he hurtled to the ground the witch made a strange gesture, pointing at her eyes with her yellow fingers and making a little circular movement. Then she burst out into terrible, screeching laughter.

Because of the witch's spell the Prince did not die when

he struck the ground. Instead he fell among thorns which pierced his eyes and blinded him. After that he wandered in the forest, eating nothing but roots and berries, and crying for his dear Rampion. For many years he strayed in misery like the poorest beggar in the land, and always he called, 'Rampion! Rampion! Sweet Rampion . . .'

But at last God took pity on the Prince and turned his feet towards the desert where Rampion lived in poverty with twins to which she had given birth. She heard the Prince calling her and embraced him and cried for joy. Two of her tears fell on the Prince's eyes and washed away the witch's spell so that his sight was given back to him. Then the Prince led his dear wife and children back to his own Kingdom where he was received with heartfelt joy, and where they lived in happiness together until they died.

As for the witch, evil came to her who had done such evil. A wolf caught her in the forest. The wolf ate every scrap of her except her yellow, clawlike hands and feet which it spat out. But the worms and beetles finished those off.

Clever Elsa

On the great plain of Hanover there was once a baker and his wife who had a daughter called Elsa. When she grew up her father said:

'Wife, it is time we had Elsa married.'

'Yes,' said his wife. 'But who will have her?'

Well, that was a problem, right enough, because her best friend would not have called Elsa pretty. But one day a young carpenter called Hans came along and said that he would marry Elsa.

'But only if she is clever,' he said.

Elsa's father dusted the flour off his apron. 'Clever?' he said. 'Clever? Listen, that girl is so clever that . . . that . . . well, she is clever, that's all I can say.'

'That's right,' said the mother. 'Our Elsa is that clever she can see the wind blowing and she can hear flies cough, so there.'

'All right,' said Hans. 'As long as she really is clever.'

The man and his wife asked Hans to stay for supper. As they sat down at the table the mother told Elsa to go into the cellar and bring beer from the barrel.

Elsa went into the cellar, tapped the barrel, put the jug

25

under the spigot, and sat down. As she was waiting for the jug to fill she looked up and saw a pickaxe, which the builders had left behind, balanced on a ledge exactly above her head.

Oh! thought Elsa. Suppose I do marry Hans, and suppose we have a baby, and the baby grows up, and I send her down here to draw beer, then the pickaxe could fall on her head and she would be killed. Aaah! Oooh! And she burst into tears.

Upstairs, the father and the mother and Hans were waiting for Elsa. Finally the father sent a servant girl into the cellar to hurry Elsa up.

The girl went down and found Elsa weeping and wailing before the barrel.

'What on earth is the matter, Elsa?' she asked. 'Have you been frightened by a big spider?'

'Noooooo,' wailed Elsa. 'But just think. If I marry Hans, and we have a child, and she grows up, and I send her down here for beer, and the pickaxe falls on her head then she will be killed. Aaaa! Eeeeeh!'

'Oh, Elsa,' said the servant girl. 'How clever you are. You are a clever Elsa for sure.' And she sat down and began weeping too.

Meanwhile the father and the mother and Hans were still waiting for their beer, so the father sent the servant lad down to the cellar. He ran down the stairs and saw Elsa and the servant girl sitting by the barrel, weeping.

'What is wrong,' the lad asked. 'Have you been frightened by a mouse?'

'Nooo,' moaned Elsa. 'But suppose I marry Hans, and we have a baby, and she grows up, and I send her down here to draw beer, and the pickaxe falls on her head then she will be killed. Aaagh! Eeegh!'

26

'I understand,' said the lad. 'What a clever Elsa you are.' And he sat down and joined in the weeping.

While this was going on the father and the mother and Hans were still waiting at the table. After a while the mother said:

'I will go down and see what is going on.'

She went into the cellar and there were Elsa, the servant girl, and the servant lad, all sitting together weeping.

'Goodness,' cried the mother. 'What is going on? Have you been frightened by a rat?'

'Nooooo,' screeched Elsa. 'But suppose I marry Hans, and we have a baby, and she grows up, and I send her down here for beer, and the pickaxe falls on her head then she will be killed. Aaaagh! Eeeegh!'

'Why that is right,' the mother said. 'What a clever Elsa you are.' And she sat down and burst out crying as well.

In the dining-room the father and Hans sat staring at the table-cloth. In the end the father could stand it no longer. He jumped up and said he would see what was happening. In the cellar he found Elsa, and the servant girl, and the servant lad, and his wife, all sitting together sobbing and sighing.

'What's up?' he shouted. 'Have you been frightened by a ghost?'

'Nooooo,' Elsa howled. 'But suppose I marry Hans, and we have a baby, and the baby grows up, and I send her down here to draw beer, and the pickaxe falls on her head then she will be killed. Aaaagh! Eeeegh!'

'That is very true,' the father cried. 'Oh, what a clever Elsa you are.' Then he sat down with the others and started crying, too.

In the dining-room Hans sat alone at the table. This is a queer do, he thought. I have never had a supper like this before. From the cellar he could hear strange sounds: moans and howls, and wails. This is amazing, he thought. I had better see for myself what is happening.

He went down the cellar stairs and found Elsa, her father, and her mother, and the servant girl and the servant lad, all weeping together by the barrel.

'Good Lord!' Hans said. 'Have you been frightened by the Devil?'

'Nooooo,' Elsa moaned. 'But, Hans, suppose we get married and have a baby, and the baby grows up and I send her down here to draw beer, and the pickaxe falls on her head, then she will be killed. Aaagh! Eeegh!'

'*Hem*,' said Hans. 'But you are right. What a clever Elsa you are. You are good enough for me, right enough.' And after he had sat down and wept he took Elsa to the church and married her.

After Hans and Clever Elsa had been married for some time, Hans said, 'Wife, we are short of money. I will go out and find work. While I am gone you go into the field and cut some corn so that we can make bread.'

Clever Elsa took her cloak and a sickle, but before she left the house she made a bowl of soup to take with her. When she reached the field she thought, What should I do first, cut the corn or eat my soup? If I cut the corn first then the soup will grow cold, so I will eat it first. What a clever Elsa I am!

She had her soup and then she thought, Now then, I ought to rest after my lunch, but should I rest first or cut the corn? If I rest first then I shall be so fresh that I will cut a lot of corn, so that is what I shall do. What a clever Elsa I am! And she lay down and went to sleep.

While Elsa was sleeping, Hans returned home. He sat by the fire and waited for his wife to get back. After three or four hours he thought, What a good wife I have. She is working so hard in the field that she does not even bother to come home for something to eat.

But when evening came Hans got worried. He went to the field, but when he got there he found Clever Elsa sound asleep with nothing in her basket, and every ear of corn had been stolen by the crows.

Hans was very cross and he decided to teach Elsa a lesson. He took a fishing-net and tied tiny bells all over it. He threw the net over Elsa then went home.

When night came, Clever Elsa woke up and stretched herself and all the little bells jingled. Elsa was startled. She jumped up and ran from the field and with every step she took the bells jingled. Elsa could not understand what was happening to her.

'Am I Clever Elsa?' she wondered. 'Am I or aren't I? I must run home and find out.'

She ran to her house but Hans had locked the door. Elsa called through the keyhole.

'Hans,' she cried. 'Is Clever Elsa there?'

'Yes,' said Hans. 'She is in bed.'

'Oh dear,' said Elsa. 'Then I am not myself!'

She ran down the village street, knocking at every door and asking, 'Who am I?' But when the villagers heard the bells tinkling they thought that she was a witch and would not answer. Then Clever Elsa ran from the village into the night and she has never been heard of since!

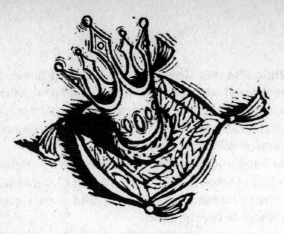

The Frog Prince

Once upon a time there was a king who had three daughters. All of them were beautiful but the youngest was the loveliest of them all. She was so beautiful that even the sun, which has seen all things since the beginning of time, even he was amazed when he shone upon her face.

Close by the King's palace there was a wood, and in the wood there was a lime tree whose scented leaves overhung a well. On hot days the young Princess liked to go into the wood and sit in the shade of the lime tree by the cool waters of the well.

The Princess had a golden ball which had been given to her by her mother, who had died years ago. When the Princess sat by the well she liked to play with her ball, throwing it into the air and clapping her hands three times before she caught it. But although the Princess did not know it, every time she sat by the well two eyes rose above the dark waters and spied on her.

One day the Princess was sitting by the well and playing with her ball. Higher and higher she threw it, until, on one throw, she lost sight of the ball in the darkness of the branches of the lime tree and as it came down it slipped through her fingers and bounced into the well.

How the Princess cried! The ball was the thing she loved most in all the world for it reminded her of her dear mother. The Princess sobbed as if her heart was breaking but, as the salt tears ran down her cheeks, she heard a 'plop!' Two eyes rose above the water in the well, and a voice croaked at her.

'Little Princess,' said the voice. 'Why do you weep so bitterly? A man with a heart of stone would pity you.'

The Princess leaned over the side of the well and saw a frog sticking its head from the water.

'Ah,' sighed the Princess, 'old water-hopper, I am crying because I have lost my golden ball in your well. I love it more than anything I possess in the whole world,' and she burst out crying again.

'Now then,' said the frog. 'Now then, now then, don't take on so. Why, I can get your ball back as easy as winking.' And he winked his big eyes one at a time just to show what he meant. 'Yes, I can get your ball, but what will you give me if I do?'

The Princess clapped her hands. 'I will give you anything,' she cried. 'I will give you my fine dresses, and my jewels, even my little golden crown!'

The frog hopped on to the well-bucket and shook his head. 'There is no need for that, my dear,' he said. 'I don't want your dresses or your jewels, and if you gave me your little golden crown then your father would be very cross. But if you will love me, and let me play with you, and if you will let me sit with you at table and eat off your little silver dish and drink from your crystal glass and sleep in your little bed then, if you promise this, I will dive down to the bottom of my well and find your golden ball.'

The Princess stared at the frog. Why, she thought, what a stupid creature this is. What can a frog do but sit in the water and croak at other frogs? How can he hope to be the friend of a human being? But the Princess was sly and she said, 'Oh, thank you, frog. I promise, indeed I do.'

The frog gave a happy croak, dived down in the green water of the well, popped up with the golden ball, and gave it to the Princess. She took it and laughed with joy, threw it up in the air, caught it, and ran off to the palace.

The frog jumped out of the well and hopped behind her. 'Wait for me,' he cried. 'Wait, my pretty one. I can't run as fast as you.'

But the Princess would not wait. She ran as fast as she could and when she got to the palace she slammed the door fast and the poor frog had to hop back to the well.

The next morning, at breakfast, the Princess was sitting at table with the King and her sisters. As she was the youngest she had to sit by the door and, halfway through her cornflakes, she heard a noise on the stairs. It was a wet squashy noise; plish, plash . . . plish, plash . . . plish, plash. Then the Princess heard a little tapping at the door and a hoarse voice cried, 'My true love, let me in!'

The Princess opened the door a crack and there was the frog, sitting at the top of the stairs goggling at her! She slammed the door shut and sat with her back to it but the King saw that she had gone pale. He put down his newspaper, pushed aside his bacon and eggs, and leaned forward.

'What is the matter, my dear?' he asked. 'Has something frightened you?'

The Princess tried to smile. 'Oh, no, father. How could I be afraid of a little frog?'

The King frowned. 'A frog? What is a frog doing in my palace?'

The Princess blushed and told her father *some* of what had happened at the well, but not her promise.

The King was angry. 'Why,' he growled, 'I will make that frog hop so fast his legs will be red hot.'

He picked up a bell to ring for his soldiers but just then there was another little knock at the door and the frog sang, in a hoarse voice:

> 'Open the door, my Princess,
> And see what you will see.
> Remember what you promised,
> Yesterday to me,
> By the cool waters of the well,
> Under the lime tree.'

'What promise is this?' asked the King, and the Princess had to tell her father *everything* that had happened by the well.

The King was not pleased with his daughter. 'What you have promised you must do,' he commanded. 'Let the frog in.'

The Princess pulled a face but the King would not allow any sulking.

'I expect the poorest peasant in the land to keep his promise,' he said. 'How much more must a princess be true to her word. Let the frog in.'

The Princess opened the door and the frog hopped in and sat by her chair, looking up through his goggly eyes.

'Lift him up,' ordered the King.

The Princess shuddered as the cold, slimy frog jumped on to her hand and she quickly spilled it on to the table. But the frog looked quite happy.

'Now, my dear,' he said. 'Please push your plate over so that we can have our breakfast together,' and he flicked out his long tongue and had a cornflake.

The Princess sat back in her chair as far as she could and it was easy to see that she did not like having a frog eating with her. But whether she liked it or not she had to do it, and she had to have her lunch and her dinner with him, too! But worse was to come.

That night the Princess had her bath. The frog did not join her because the water was too hot, but when the Princess went to her bedroom there, squatting on the marble floor of the corridor, the frog was waiting for her.

'Now, my dear,' said the frog, 'I am tired with hopping about this huge palace all day. Take me into your bedroom and put me in your little bed and we will lie down and go to sleep.'

The Princess began to cry because she certainly did not want to have a damp frog in bed with her, but the King was stern.

'The frog helped you,' he said. 'You must not turn your back on him now. Take him in.'

The Princess picked up the frog with two fingers, carried him into the bedroom, and dropped him in a corner. But no sooner had she got into bed than the frog came across the floor. Splish, splash, squish, squash, he hopped nearer and nearer and then, with a huge leap, he jumped on to the bed and sat on the pillow.

The Princess felt his clammy head against her neck and she jumped up with a squeal.

'Ah!' she squeaked as she saw the frog sitting in a pool

of water on her satin pillow. 'You nasty brute.' She seized the frog by the back leg and threw it across the room. 'Now lie there, and I hope that the cat gets you tomorrow and eats you up.'

The poor frog lay quite still and looked at the Princess through sad eyes. It tried to move but it could only twitch its legs. It opened its mouth and tried to speak, but only a sigh came from its lips. Just once it shook its head and then its eyes began to close in death.

The Princess jumped out of bed and ran to the frog. When she saw its bruised little body, and its sad, dim eyes, she felt pity for it, and remorse. For the frog did not seem a damp creature which filled her with disgust, but just another poor, battered animal which was suffering because of a human being's cruelty.

'Poor frog,' she sighed. 'I am truly sorry. Forgive me,' and she picked him up and, out of pity and love, she kissed him.

But even as she kissed the frog her eyes grew big and round, for the frog was changing! His skin turned from green to yellow to white to pink; his front legs grew longer and his back legs grew shorter, and in the twinkling of an eye he turned into a fine young man with a kind face.

This time the Princess really screamed. She screamed so loudly that she nearly brought the house down. The King and his soldiers came running into the room and grabbed the young man. But he held up his arms.

'It is all right,' he said. 'I am not a thief who has broken in. I am the frog changed back into my true shape. Yes, long ago a witch put a spell on me because my father, who is a king, stopped her frightening people. She turned me into a frog and threw me down the well and said that I would never be a prince again until a princess kissed me.'

He turned to the Princess. 'And you have done that, Your Highness,' he said. 'Although you were cruel to me at first yet, in the end, you felt love for me, even though you thought that I was ugly and nasty. Yes, the goodness of your heart showed through in the end.'

The next day the Prince asked the King if he could marry the Princess. The King was delighted and agreed, but only if his daughter agreed, too. She did, because she had fallen in love with her Frog Prince, and the marriage was arranged for a week next Wednesday. The Prince sent into his own land, and a coach and four white horses came to drive him to the church for the wedding.

The coach was driven by the Prince's own true servant, Faithful Henry. Henry walked stiffly and could not bend down because when his master had been turned into a frog he had got a blacksmith to bind three iron bands around his chest, in case his heart should burst with grief. But as he drove the Prince to the church there was a wrenching sound. The Prince thought that the carriage had broken down, but when he leaned forward he saw that one of the iron bands had cracked and fallen off Henry. Twice more there was a wrenching sound, and each time it was an iron band falling from the faithful lad, and so he was free to jump and leap like any other young man. Then the Frog Prince and the Princess were married and lived happily ever after.

So all turned out well, although not the well the Prince had lived in!

Tom Thumb

A farm-worker and his wife lived by the edge of a forest. Although they were poor, and the farmer the man worked for was harsh, they were happy. But one autumn night, as they were sitting together, the man lit his pipe, leaned back in his chair, and said, 'How quiet our house is.'

His wife looked up from her sewing. 'Yes,' she said, 'it is quiet.'

And indeed the house was quiet. The only sounds were the rain tapping on the window and the ticking of the clock.

The man leaned forward and poked the fire. 'It is sad that we have no children,' he said. 'A child would brighten up our lives. Other people's houses, where they have a family, are so cheerful.'

His wife stared into the flames of the fire. 'Yes,' she agreed. 'Why, even if we had only one child, and if it was no bigger than my thumb, still, I would be content then; and we would love it with all our hearts.'

'That we would,' said the man. 'That we would. Well, let us live in hope.'

37

A year or so went by and their hope was rewarded for the woman did have a child, and it was almost as though her words had been heard by the spirits of the forest; for the child was only as big as her thumb! But although the baby was tiny it was strong and healthy, and it looked at the world through bright, clever eyes.

'Well,' said the man, 'your wish has come true.'

'It has,' the woman said. She held the baby in the palm of her hand and smiled at it. 'Yes, and it is as dear to me as any child could be.'

And that was true. The man and the woman were well content with their little child, and because it was so tiny they called it Tom Thumb.

The years passed away and Tom made the house cheerful as he played by the fire like a bright cricket, and helped his mother do the housework by polishing the knives and forks with a little duster. And, although in all those years Tom did not grow as much as a hair's breadth, still he was loved and cherished.

One day, when Tom was about ten, his father had to go into the forest and cut wood. All morning he chopped wood, loaded it on to a cart, and dragged it back to the house leading the horse by the reins. At noon, when he was having bread and sausages in the house, he said, 'Oh, I wish that I had a helper who could do the driving for me. I could get on with the wood-cutting then and have it finished in half the time.'

Tom looked up from his tiny chair on the table. 'I'll do that for you, Dad,' he chirped.

His father smiled down at Tom. 'That's very nice of you, Tom,' he said, 'but I don't think that you could do it. You are so little that you could not even hold the reins, let alone guide the horse.'

'That's all right,' Tom answered, and his bright eyes sparkled with cleverness. 'Just you put me in the horse's ear and I will tell it what to do.'

'Well . . .' the farmer rubbed his chin. 'It's worth a try. All right, I'll go off to the forest and you can follow me in half an hour or so.'

The father went off to the woods, and after a while Tom's mother put him in the horse's ear.

Tom grabbed the long hairs inside the ear and shouted, 'Gee up, Dobbin.'

The good old horse nodded his head and set off and it did exactly what Tom told it to do, stopping when he shouted 'Whoa,' starting when he called 'Gee up,' and turning left and right as if it knew the way by heart. Across the fields they went, on to the rough pasture, and then, as they were crossing a bridge, they came upon two idlers lounging against the parapet.

Hidden inside the horse's ear, Tom called, 'Come on, Dobbin. Over the bridge.'

The two idlers were amazed. 'What's this?' one cried. 'Here is a horse and cart with a driver guiding it but the driver is invisible!'

'You're right,' said the other man. 'Let's follow the horse and see what's up.'

Dobbin plodded on and after a little while he, and the cart, and Tom, arrived at the wood pile. Tom leaned out of the horse's ear.

'Hello, Dad,' he called. 'Here we are, safe and sound.'

Tom's father was delighted. He took Tom from Dobbin's ear and placed him down and the little lad sat on a dock leaf and swung his legs, as pleased as his father. But the two loafers were spying through the trees.

'Do you see that?' said the first one. 'A tiny boy!

Listen, if we could get hold of him we could show him in a freak show and make a fortune. Let's see if we can snatch him.'

The other man agreed and they slouched from the trees and went up to Tom's father.

'Hey!' they called. 'How about selling that little fellow, there?'

Tom's father shook his head. 'Sell my own son?' he cried. 'Never, not for all the gold in Germany.'

One of the men spat sideways. 'What's your worry?' he said. 'We'll look after him, don't worry about that. Anyway, it will be good for him, he'll get about, travel, see the world.'

'No,' said Tom's father. 'And that's definite. That lad is dearer to me than the whole world. Now clear off.' And just to make his point he swung his axe over his shoulder.

The two men looked at him; but although Tom was tiny his father was big and strong and the axe was sharp, so they just shrugged.

'All right, then,' they said. 'Don't lose your hair,' and they made to clear off. But Tom had heard the offer and he climbed up his father's coat and whispered in his ear.

'Now, Dad,' he whispered. 'Take the money. Go on, sell me. I won't be away for long. I'll get away from those two men before you can say Jack Robinson.'

Tom's father was not happy about selling his son but he knew that Tom was quick-witted, and so, reluctantly, he agreed. The two idlers were delighted. They handed over a piece of gold which they had stolen the day before and plucked Tom from his father's shoulder.

'Now where shall we put you?' the first man said.

Tom grinned. 'Put me on the brim of your hat. I'll be safe there and I can see the world as we walk along.'

The man put Tom on his hat brim and they set off to the nearest town. As dusk drew in Tom shouted to the man:

'Let me down. Put me on the ground.'

The man shook his head and nearly knocked Tom flying. 'No, no,' he said. 'You just stay up there.'

'I've got to get down,' Tom called. 'I want to widdle!'

'Widdle up there,' growled the man. 'My hat has had worse than that on it.'

Tom stamped his feet. 'No,' he shouted. 'I know my manners. I was brought up properly. Put me down.'

The man could not bear Tom's squeaking any longer.

'All right,' he said. 'Just for a minute.' And he put his hat on the ground. Tom jumped off the hat and slipped through a hedge into a field. He dodged about among the sods and then slipped down a mouse-hole. As loudly as he could, he shouted. 'Goodnight, gents. Off you go to the freak show, but you can go without me!'

The two men cursed and swore. They charged into the field looking for Tom. They poked a stick down the mouse-hole but Tom just crept in deeper and lay there out of harm's way. Soon it got dark and the two idlers had to give up their search and slope off, their pockets empty but their hearts full of rage!

Tom heard the thunder of their feet as they stormed off and he crept out of the mouse-hole. There was no moon to see by and Tom stumbled about the field, tripping over pebbles and grass roots.

My word, Tom thought, I could break my neck here. But after a while, he found an empty snail-shell. 'Now

41

that's just the job,' he said to himself. 'I will spend the night in there.'

He plucked two petals from a dogrose and made a bed for himself and snuggled inside the shell. Just as he was falling asleep two burglars came creeping across the meadow. They stopped near Tom and he heard them talking.

'Now, Bill,' one said in a coarse voice. 'Where shall we go burgling?'

'Well,' said Bill, 'the parson is rich. His cook told me that the parlour is stuffed with silver and gold. The trouble is that he is so mean he has bars all over the place, so how can we get in?'

Tom sat up in bed. 'I can tell you,' he shouted.

The two burglars nearly jumped out of their skins. 'Who's that?' they cried. 'Who's that?'

'It's me,' Tom said and burst out laughing.

The burglars looked around but they could not see anything. Bill thought that there was a ghost about and wanted to run away but Tom told them to strike a match. By its light they saw Tom peeping out of the snail-shell.

'Well I'll be blowed,' Bill said. 'A tiny lad. How can a little shrimp like you help us?'

'That's easy,' Tom said. 'Just put me through the bars on the parson's window and I'll pass out anything you want. I'm stronger than I look.' And he flexed his arm so that a muscle about as big as a pea showed.

The burglars didn't think much of Tom's muscle but they liked his idea so they picked him up and padded off to the parson's house. When they got there they pushed Tom through the bars, but the minute he was inside he cried out with all his might.

'Do you want everything in here?'

The burglars peered through the window. 'Shush,' they whispered. 'You'll wake up the whole house.'

Tom heard them but he didn't pay any attention. He skipped across the table and shouted again. 'What about these knives and forks? They're silver, and here is a gold candlestick. Do you want that?'

The burglars rolled their eyes. 'Shush, shush. Be serious,' they hissed, but Tom just dashed about the table, kicking the cups and saucers on to the floor and rattling the egg cups. He made such a din that he woke the cook who slept in the next room. She sat up in bed with her hair in curlers, listened to the racket next door, and screamed, 'Master, master, the burglars are in the house!' Then she fainted.

The burglars heard her scream and legged it for all they were worth and Tom slipped through the bars, climbed down a tendril of ivy, and ran into the cowshed, and hid in the manger. There he was warm and comfortable as he snuggled into the hay ready for a good night's sleep and looking forward to getting home to his mother and father the next day.

But, as they say, don't count your chickens before they are hatched; there is always plenty of trouble waiting for you in this world as Tom soon found out because the next morning the herdsman came in to feed the cows and the very first armful of hay he picked up was the one in which Tom was sleeping! Before Tom knew what was happening he was in the mouth of a hungry cow!

Tom woke up and saw a row of huge yellow teeth chomping away. 'I'm in a fulling mill,' he cried, and he jumped about on the cow's tongue hoping not to be ground up into a paste and trying to dart out of the cow's mouth. But it was no good. In the end the cow gave a big gollop and down Tom slid into its stomach.

Poor Tom was so confused that he thought that he had been pushed into a dungeon. He rolled around, trying to climb back up the cow's throat, but every time he did so the cow swallowed more fodder and back Tom tumbled. More and more hay came down until he was almost crushed. At last he yelled, 'No more hay. No more hay.'

Now the milkmaid had just come in to milk the cow and, as she sat on her stool with her cheek pressed against the cow's side, she heard Tom's voice. She screamed and jumped up, spilling the milk, and ran into the house screeching, 'The cow is bewitched. Its stomach is talking!'

The parson was reading the paper over his breakfast. He looked up sternly and frowned. 'Don't talk nonsense. How can a cow's stomach talk? You must be drunk.'

'No I'm not,' said the maid. 'Come and listen for yourself.'

The parson slapped his paper down, strode out to the cowshed, put his head against the cow's side and, sure enough, he heard Tom's voice calling, 'No more hay, no more hay!'

The parson looked at the herdsman, and the dairymaid, and they looked at him.

'The cow is bewitched,' said the herdsman. 'You must kill it.'

'Yes, kill it,' cried the dairymaid.

Now, it is all very well to jump about shouting 'Kill the cow' if the cow isn't yours; if it is, it is quite another matter. That is what the parson thought, anyway, and so he ran into the church and got some holy water and splashed it over the cow's head.

'Now then,' he cried. 'Come out, you devil.'

But Tom couldn't get out of the cow. He was up to his neck in half-chewed hay and nearly suffocated. All he could do was shout, 'No more hay, no more hay!'

The parson sprinkled a gallon of holy water all over the cow but still the little voice kept piping away, so in the end he ordered the cow to be slaughtered and walked away with tears in his eyes.

The butcher came and killed the poor cow and cut it up. As nobody wanted the cow's stomach it was thrown on to the rubbish heap with Tom inside it. Tom kicked and pushed and struggled, trying to get out of the stomach, and then, just as he had squeezed his head out, a hungry wolf jumped into the farmyard and swallowed the stomach in one gulp.

Well, thought Tom, it isn't my day. I'm out of the frying-pan and into the fire! But he did not despair. He lay in the stomach thinking hard, even though he was jogged up and down as the wolf ran back to the forest. Then Tom had an idea. 'Wolf,' he called. 'Wolf, I know where you can get the best meal you have ever had in your entire life; bacon and sausages and pies—and all for free!'

The wolf stopped running. 'Oh,' he said, licking his lips. 'Where is that?'

'It is on the edge of the forest,' Tom said, and he described his father's house. 'There is a grating over the store-room window but a bit was broken off it and you will be able to squeeze through. Just think—pies, sausages, bacon, and—'

But the wolf did not stop to hear any more, it set off and ran like the wind all the way to Tom's home. That night it found the grating and squeezed through the hole

45

and gorged itself on the food in the store-room. When it had eaten everything it could find it tried to get out again but it had become so fat that it could not get through the hole.

Tom had reckoned on this and he began to jump about inside the wolf. The wolf didn't like that. It jumped about as if it was being tickled inside and made such a commotion that Tom's father and mother were woken up. They peeped through a crack in the door. 'It's a wolf,' whispered Tom's father. 'A mad wolf!'

They tiptoed away and got an axe and a scythe. Then they crept back and stood outside the door. 'When I say "go",' said Tom's father, 'you attack the wolf with the scythe and I'll attack it with the axe. Now, go!'

They both dashed into the room, and before the wolf could so much as open its mouth to bite them, the woman had struck it with the scythe and the man had hit it with the axe and so it fell down dead.

Tom felt the wolf fall over and he ended up standing on his head. But he called out, 'Father, Mother, here I am, inside the wolf.'

Tom's mother ran into the sitting-room for a pair of scissors and cut open the wolf, and Tom popped out as fresh as a daisy.

'Ah!' said his father. 'Ah, my dear son. You have only been away a night and a day, but what sorrow and misery we have been through, worrying about you.'

Tom plucked some damp hay from his collar. 'Yes, Dad,' he said. 'I must say that I have knocked about a bit since then, and been knocked about, too. Phoo—thank goodness I can breathe some fresh air again.'

His mother picked Tom up and brushed him down. 'Where on earth have you been?' she asked.

'Why,' said Tom, 'I have been down a mouse-hole, in a cow's stomach, in the paunch of a wolf—but I am back home now and I shan't wander far again, I can tell you.'

'That you won't,' cried his mother. 'We would not sell you again for all the money in the world.'

Then Tom had his supper, and a bath in an egg cup, and slept in his tiny cot, and never roamed away from home again.

The King of the Hedges

I n olden times, when, as the Good Book says, all men earned their bread by the sweat of their brow, everything in the world could speak. Yes, everything, and every sound had a meaning. When the blacksmith smote the glowing iron on his forge, his hammer spoke: 'Strike hard, Master,' it called, in a voice as deep and clanging as the great bell of Munster cathedral. 'Aye, strike hard!'

And when the carpenter planed down rough timber to turn it into smooth planks, his plane said, in a grating voice, 'Here goes . . . here goes,' and the timber answered, 'Oh yes, here goes. Ooh! Yes, here goes!'

The great mill-wheel spoke, too. As the green waters of the mill-stream turned it around it clattered away and said, in a pious way, like a parson on Sunday, 'Aid me, Lord God. Aid me, Lord God.' And if the miller was a thief who stole flour from the peasants who brought him their wheat to be ground down, then, if the miller was away and could not turn off the water, it groaned, slowly, 'Who . . . is . . . there? Who . . . is . . . there?' And then it would answer itself quickly, 'The-miller. The-miller, the-miller,'

And then, very quickly, it creaked, 'Ohwhatathiefheis-Ohwhatathiefheis-Hestealsthreepecksfromeverybushel!'

In those good old days the birds, too, had their own language which all men understood. Nowadays, alas, it sounds just like chirping and screeching, piping and twittering, although, even now, to those with ears to hear it, it is music without words, like a violin concerto.

Of course, in those innocent times, just as men could understand the birds, so could the birds understand the language of men. The birds knew, very well, that men had kings who ruled over them and made laws, and so the birds decided that they, too, would have a king, hoping that by his rule he would bring happiness among them, although who knows whether kings do that or not?

All the birds agreed to this except the green plover. He had been born free, and had lived free, and he wished to die free, too. When he heard the birds' decision he flew anxiously here and there, crying, 'Where shall I go? Where shall I go?' Until he came to a remote and lonely marsh where he lived a solitary and quiet life, and still does.

However, the other birds decided to have a meeting to decide who would be their king and, one fine May morning, they gathered together from the woods and the fields and the sea-shore. They were all there: eagles and chaffinches, owls and crows, larks and sparrows, but how can a simple story-teller name them all? Even the elusive cuckoo was there and the hoopoe, with his beautiful crest, who is called the cuckoo's clerk because he always arrives a few days before the cuckoo. And, as well, there was another bird present, a tiny brown creature, no bigger than a mouse, which did not even have a name of its own to bless itself with.

As all the birds gathered, a cock and his hen wandered on to the meadow. The hen, which had not heard about the great meeting, was amazed and frightened. 'What? What?' she cackled. 'What is going on? What is going on?' But the cock calmed his dear wife. 'Now then,' he crowed. 'Don't fret yourself. It is only a lot of rich folk who are going to choose a king.'

After the birds had settled down they began their conference. It was just like any other conference. Every bird present had its own idea about who should be king, and every one of them wanted to have its say. What a din there was; whistling and crying and piping and peeping and croaking and hooting! It sounded more like Bedlam than a conference. But at last a magpie had an idea.

'Let our King be the bird which can fly the fastest,' it rattled.

Some of the birds liked that idea, but others thought that it was not fair.

'After all,' said the woodpecker, 'who can fly faster than the swift? And who flies slower than the heron? We might just as well make the swift our King straightaway.'

The birds had to agree with that for, after all, who is faster than the swift, with its curved and swooping wings?

'All right then,' the magpie rasped. 'Let some other bird think of a better idea,' and it fluttered into a tree and sulked behind a branch.

Then the swan, which is usually silent until the hour of its death, spoke. 'Let our King be the bird which can fly the highest,' it hissed.

The birds liked that suggestion, all except the ostrich. 'That isn't fair, either,' he called. 'I can't fly at all.'

'Well,' chirped the robin, 'in that case you aren't a bird!'

The ostrich was so offended by that remark that he stalked off in a huff and stuck his head in the ground. But the other birds liked the idea and, anyway, they did not want to hang around debating all day, and so they whistled and screeched, 'Yes, yes, let the bird which can fly the highest be our King.'

But nearby, in some bushes, was a tree-frog. He shook his head and croaked, 'No, no, do not do it.' He was a wise old frog and knew that many tears would flow because of the contest. However, the crow wagged his black head and cawed, 'Yes, yes. It is quite all right. Everything will go smoothly.'

And so it was agreed and the birds decided to start there and then, while it was still early in the day, so that every bird would have plenty of time to fly as high as it could, and no bird would have an excuse to go around afterwards grumbling that it could have flown the highest if only it had been given more time.

The birds began to get ready. They stretched their wings and preened their feathers and waited for the signal, which was to be given by the cock, which has the loudest cry of all the birds. The cock stretched his neck and fluttered into the air to make sure that there was no cheating, and then, as his wife gazed at him adoringly, he took a deep breath:

'Get ready,' he crowed. 'Ready, steady, cock-a-doodle GO!'

All the birds flew into the air. There were so many wings beating that dust rose from the meadow; there was such a huge fluttering and beating of feathers that it looked as if a vast, black cloud was rising from the earth.

Up went the birds, higher and higher, above the cottages, over the church steeple, above the trees and the hills; up they flew, their eyes bulging and their beaks gaping. Soon the little birds, the sparrows and warblers and finches, began to tire and they dropped down to the meadow. The bigger birds, the owls and the geese and the hawks, held out longer, straining to fly as high as they possibly could and so to win the crown, but none of them could fly as high as the noble eagle who soared up until he could have plucked out the burning eye of the sun.

When the eagle had risen above all the other birds he peered down on them and thought, Well, I have gone high enough. None of those measly birds can possibly reach me so why should I bother going higher? So he rested, gliding on his magnificent wings as all the birds cried, 'Yes, mighty eagle, you have won. You must be our King. No other bird can fly as high as you.'

But as the eagle bowed its head graciously, a tiny voice screeched, 'Ah ha! No other bird but me!' And the little brown bird without a name crept from the eagle's feathers, where he had been hiding; and as he had stolen a free lift, he was not tired at all and he beat his little wings so furiously that he ended up perching on God's own footstool. From there he looked down and cried in a loud voice:

'Aha, aha! I am the King. Yes, I am King of all the birds of the air!'

But the other birds were furious. 'You our King?' they screamed. 'Never! Never! You have only reached God's footstool by cheating. No, we will have another test.'

The birds gathered again in the meadow and this time they decided that their king would be the bird which could get *lowest* to the ground.

All the birds tried to get as low down as they could. The goose, with its broad breast flopped about in the dust, and the hen scratched away to make a hole in the ground for her husband, the cock. It was funny to see although you can feel sorry for the poor duck. He jumped into a ditch but sprained his legs and had to waddle to a pond, quacking, 'Cheating! cheating!'

It was a strange sight, but the little brown bird without a name was cunning. He crept into a mouse-hole and cried, 'I am lower than any other bird. I am the King. I am the King.'

How angry the other birds were. 'You our King?' they called. 'Never in a million years! Do you think that we will let you get away with cheating?' They crowded around the mouse-hole. 'Come out,' they cried. 'Come out and take your punishment.'

The little bird was frightened when he heard that. He crouched inside the hole and would not come out.

'Very well then,' said the birds. 'Stay down there. Stay down there until you starve. You are our prisoner. We will teach you a lesson, you little cheat.'

It was nearly evening by then and, after their great contest, the birds were tired and wanted to get back to their nests, and some of them had nestlings which needed looking after. So, because he stays awake all night long, anyway, they made the owl their sentry.

'Guard the mouse-hole,' they told the owl. 'Don't let the little villain get away, not if you value your life.' Then they all flew away to trees, or hedges, or bushes, wherever they had made their nests.

And so, as the sun set, the owl was left alone, standing before the mouse-hole. He stood up very straight and stared at the hole with his huge, yellow eyes. But he was tired, too. After all he had flown high that day, higher than he had ever flown before because, as a rule, owls do not fly very high.

After a little while the owl yawned and he thought, Well, I can close one eye. With the other I will watch the hole and if that little bird so much as pokes his beak out I will snatch him with my huge claws.

The owl closed his left eye and at once the little brown bird darted from the mouse-hole but the owl grabbed at him and he jumped back into the hole. Then the owl closed his right eye and opened his left eye. Every ten minutes he closed one eye and opened the other, but there came a time when he closed one eye and forgot to open the other, and as soon as both his eyes were closed he fell sound asleep! The little bird heard the owl snore, slipped from the mouse-hole, and got clean away.

From that time, when every sound had its own meaning, the owl has never dared to appear in daylight. If he does the other birds mob him and pluck out his feathers. So now the owl flies at night, calling, 'Hoo hoo, tu wit to huu,' as he floats in the moonlight on silent wings, looking, with his huge eyes, for mice to kill, for he hates them because they make holes.

The little bird hides, too. He skulks about the hedges, or flits quickly across any open glades, because he knows that if the other birds see him he will be killed for cheating and escaping. But still, if he is hidden and thinks that he is safe, you will hear him shout, in a surprisingly loud voice, 'I am the King. Yes, I am the King of the Birds.' Because of this the other birds call him, in mockery, '*Zaunkönig*', which in German means 'King of the Hedges', although in England we call the little bird Jenny Wren.

But, in fact, the birds were quite happy that they did not have a king and none of them was happier than the skylark. And to this day, as soon as the sun rises he ascends into the heavens and hovers over the fields and, joyful in his freedom, he sings, 'Ah, how beautiful the heavens and the earth are. How beautiful, how beautiful, how beautiful.'

If you go into the country on a fine spring morning you will hear the lark singing, and you will hear the King of the Hedges rattling away. And, if you wait until dusk, when the white moths begin to glimmer in the darkness, you will hear the owl hooting as he hunts for his enemies, the mice.

Look and Listen!

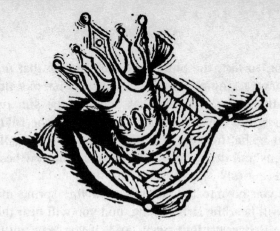

The Giant Turnip

T here were two brothers from Kassel who served in the army for seven years. While they were in the army the elder brother thieved and stole and plundered everything he could lay his hands on, but the second brother served his time like a good and honourable soldier should, doing his duty and stealing nothing.

When they left the army the Colonel said what a good soldier the younger brother had been, and what a bad soldier the elder brother had been, but for all that the elder brother was rich and the younger brother was as poor as a church mouse.

The rich brother built himself a fine house and lived like a prince, but the poor brother had to rent a worn out acre of land and scrape a living from that.

One day as the rain and sleet lashed down, an old beggar woman came hobbling down the road. She stopped at the rich brother's house and asked for food and shelter but he told her to clear off or he would set the dogs on her. Then the old woman went to the poor brother and he let her stay in his hut and shared with her what little he had. When the old woman left, she pointed at the field.

'Plant turnips,' she said, and went on her way.

The next spring the poor brother remembered what the old woman had said. He dug his bit of land and hoed it and sowed the whole field with turnip seed. After a few weeks the turnips began to grow and in the middle of the field one grew as big as a football. But when the other turnips stopped growing this turnip kept on. Bigger and bigger it grew, swelling as the poor brother watched it, so that it might have been called the king of turnips for never had such a one been seen before, and such a one will never be seen again.

So there in the middle of the field loomed the gigantic turnip, but the poor brother had no idea what to do with it. Then a neighbour said:

'Look here, that is the king of turnips, so why not take it to the King? You never know, he might buy it. It's worth a try, anyway, because no one else is likely to want it.'

Well, as the man had said it was worth a try, so the poor brother loaded it on a cart and took it to the King and it took eight oxen to pull the cart. When the King saw the turnip he was delighted.

'What a marvellous turnip,' he cried. 'I have never seen such a monster in all my days.'

He called out his Queen and his children and they laughed and clapped their hands when they saw the enormous turnip.

'Tell me,' said the King to the poor brother, 'who are you? Are you a child of good fortune?'

'No,' said the poor brother. 'Your Majesty, I am an old soldier and I am so poor that I don't have two pennies to rub together. I have a rich brother who is well known, but because I am poor I am forgotten by everyone.'

'Well,' said the King, 'we must do something about

that,' and he gave the poor brother fields and meadows and herds of cows and money in plenty, so that the poor brother became rich, and much richer than his brother.

When the rich brother heard this news he was green with envy and wondered how he could become richer himself. Then he hit upon a cunning plan. He got a cart and put everything he possessed on it. Yes; every piece of gold and silver he had, all his furniture, all his fine linen sheets, and every knife, fork, and spoon. Then he set off to the King's palace. For, he thought, if my brother got all his wealth in return for a turnip, then if I give the King all these magnificent things, what will he not give me in return?

The rich brother got to the palace and asked to see the King. When the King came out the rich brother said:

'Your Majesty, I love and admire you so much that I have come to give you all these splendid presents.'

'Thank you,' said the King. 'That is very nice of you. Now I shall give you a present in return, but what shall I give you? Obviously you have everything you need or you would not give me all these expensive things.'

The King rubbed his beard for a moment or two and then his eyes lit up.

'I know,' he cried. 'The perfect gift!'

And he gave the brother the turnip.

The Carrion Crows

There was a poor lad, once, who could not find a job, so he joined up as a soldier. There were some ruffians in the army in those days; worthless rogues who idled their time away gambling and loafing in taverns. But that's the way it was. After all, who would join up to live in a bare barracks and be cursed at by sergeants, and maybe to have his arms and legs blown off, unless he could find nothing better to do?

But there were some decent men in the army and this lad was one of them. He did his duty, kept himself clean, and did not spend too much time in taverns. His idea was that he would save up his pay until he could buy himself a small shop, and then he would settle down with a good wife.

Now in this man's regiment there were two villains. Yes, they were two false hearted rogues, but they were crafty, as well. They knew that the soldier had money saved up and they wanted it for themselves.

They began to butter up the soldier. Every day they would say, 'Hello, mate, come and have a drink with us,' or, 'Here, chum, have a slice of this nice sausage. Go on,

we're always ready to share with a decent lad like you.'
They were two sly villains!

As time passed the three men became friends—at least
the good soldier thought so. Then the two villains began
to talk about leaving the army. 'We can't leave,' they said.
'We haven't got any money. But you have. Why don't
you get your savings from the Colonel and clear out? Why
stay here to be cursed like a dog when you can get out
and enjoy yourself while you're still young?'

The soldier thought about this and one day he said,
'You lads are right. I'm getting out of this mob. I'm going
to leave next week.'

The two villains slapped the soldier on the back and
said what a fine sensible lad he was. 'That's it,' they said.
'Get out while the going's good. And don't forget to take
your savings out.'

The next week was Easter Week, and on Good Friday
the soldier handed over his kit and his musket, picked up
his savings, saluted the Colonel for the last time, and left
the barracks. At the gate the two villains were waiting for
him. 'We'll walk with you for a bit,' they said. 'Just to
see you safely on to the high road.'

They walked on for a while until they came to a
crossroads where there was a gallows on which a poor
sinner had been hanged.

'Why do they hang murderers at crossroads?' the
soldier asked.

'Ah,' said one of the villains. 'That is so that the dead
man's ghost won't know which way to go to haunt the
people who hanged him.'

'Is that the reason?' The soldier nodded. 'Still, we
aren't ghosts and we know which way to go. We turn
left.'

'No we don't,' said the villains. 'We turn right.'

The soldier looked to the right and saw that the road led into the forest where only wolves and bears lived. 'No,' he said. 'That's no good.'

Now this was just what the villains wanted the soldier to say because they were looking for an excuse to have a row. One of them pushed his ugly face against the soldier's nose.

'Are you calling me a liar?' he demanded.

The soldier took a step backwards. 'Of course not,' he said.

'Oh yes you are!' The villain pretended to fly into a rage. 'No one calls me a liar,' he shouted, and he hit the soldier.

Well, the soldier was no coward. He clouted the villain back and nearly knocked his brains out. But the other villain picked up a stick and hit the soldier on the back of the head. The soldier fell down and the two villains beat him and kicked him. Yes, the cowards beat the soldier without mercy. In fact they beat him so badly that they thought he was dead. Then they took his savings and went to the town where they spent the money in taverns.

But the soldier was a strong man, and although he was badly hurt he was still alive. He lay on the path and the setting sun shone down on him, and the evening star twinkled through the pine trees of the forest; but the poor soldier could not see the setting sun, nor the evening star.

'How dark the night is!' he cried. On his hands and knees he crawled about the muddy path. 'Mother!' he called. 'Mother!' But the only answer he got was from a thrush singing the evening away.

The soldier heard the thrush and knew that it was still

evening, and then he knew that he was blinded. 'Oh God,' he cried, 'have pity on me.'

Through the mud he crawled, blood oozing from his head and his eyes, and then his bruised hands touched the gallows. He grasped the post and dragged himself up, and spread out his hands on high and touched the cross-beam whereon the poor sinner had been hanged.

'Ah,' whispered the soldier, 'God is with me yet. For this is a blessed cross, like that on which the Saviour of the world was crucified. Aye, like that on which Jesus was nailed, giving his blood and his life to redeem a poor lost soul like me.'

And then, like Christ himself, he groaned and sweated a bloody sweat and fainted.

Dusk came and, between the setting of the sun and the rising of the moon, as wolves began to wail, and as owls began to open their huge eyes, and as poor men blew out their rushlights, and as rich men lit their candles, three carrion crows, as black as soot, came fluttering in from the fields and perched on the cross-beam of the gallows.

The crows folded their wings and gripped the beam with their scaly claws. 'Aowk,' they croaked. 'Aowk, aowk,' and they turned their heads this way and that, their bright eyes searching for any enemies, stoats or weasels, which might be lurking by. But they saw no enemies, no stoats or weasels lurking by, and they did not see the poor soldier lying bleeding under the gallows.

The crows preened their feathers with their savage beaks and then, rested and preened, as the sun blinked its last goodnight and the badgers of the forest snuffled from their setts, the first crow spoke.

'Krah,' it called. 'Krah. Sisters, you have flown many a mile today. What good news do you bring?'

The second crow wagged its dark and dangerous beak. 'Kaw,' it called. 'Kaw. Today I flew across the town and, do you know, sisters, there is no water there. It is true, the humans are dying of thirst and yet in the market square there is a stone, and under that stone there is a well, and in that well there is a stream with water enough for ten thousand people. If only men knew what we know!'

The crows laughed, 'Aowk, aowk, aowk.' They clicked their beaks and shifted from claw to claw as the soldier lay, unseen, beneath them.

Then the third crow spoke. 'Hurrgh. Hurrgh,' it went, clearing its throat of beetles' legs. 'What do men know, the ignorant fools! Sisters, the old King's daughter is sick unto death. Yes, she is dying and no man can cure her. The King has said that any man who can save her may marry her and be a prince. But no man knows how to save her and so she will die. Hurrgh! If only men knew what we know. In the mill-pond there is a toad and if that toad is burned into ashes and the Princess takes the ashes then she will be cured. But no man knows that and so she will die!'

'Krah,' called the first crow. 'Krah. How clever man thinks he is. He sees the secrets of the stars and the mysteries of the earth and yet he does not know that there is a well in his town or that a toad will cure the Princess. Krah. Sisters, today I saw a blind man fall down a well. Krah. He tumbled right down it and drowned. I saw him as I flew to the field where the wire-worms are. I had a good feed there, sisters.'

The crows raised their heads and wagged their beaks in mocking laughter. 'Aowk, aowk,' they laughed as the bats flitted across the yellow moon.

'Krah,' said the first crow. 'If only that blind man had

known that under this gallows the dew, which falls from Heaven, will wash away all blindness he would not be dead in a well tonight with newts and frogs crawling over him. If only men knew what we know.'

'Kaw,' the second crow nodded. 'The humans think that they are wise, and yet people die of thirst, the Princess is dying, and men go blind, but still they kill us who would tell all if we were left in peace. Well, let us sleep, sisters, tomorrow we must fly to the pasture where the beetles live.'

'Krah,' said the first crow. 'And the stupid humans will try to kill us who eat their enemies . . .'

But the other crows had fallen asleep and so the first crow put her head under her wing and slept, too.

And as the crows slept the soldier crept from under the gallows and gathered dew and drenched his poor eyes. And when he looked up he saw all the stars of Heaven shining down on him.

The next morning the soldier hurried to the mill-pond and caught the ancient toad which lived there. He burned the toad to ashes and then ran to the old King's palace.

'Your Majesty,' he said. 'I am only a poor, ignorant soldier, but if you put this toad ash into a broth and give it to your daughter, the Princess, she will be cured.'

The King did not like the idea of his daughter drinking the ashes of a toad, but the Queen sent for the cook and he made a broth. The Princess pulled a face but she drank it, and it was just as the crows had said, she was cured.

But the King did not like the look of the soldier. His clothes were torn and muddy and his face was cut and bruised so that he looked like a beggar who had been driven from pillar to post.

I can't let a vagabond like this marry my daughter, he thought; but he did not dare to say so because he had given his word, and if he broke it, then he knew that his people would be angry and would drag him from his throne. He thought for a while and then he said:

'You can marry my daughter but only on this condition. The people in my town are dying of thirst. If you can find enough water for them then you can marry my daughter.'

The King thought that he was clever in saying that because he was sure that the soldier could not find water for the town. But the soldier remembered what the crows had said. He went to the market square, lifted up a stone, and under the stone was a well, and in the well was a spring of pure water, enough to quench the thirst of ten thousand people.

Well, the King was not too pleased but he had to stand by his word and so the soldier married the Princess and lived in a palace of his own and he was well loved by the people.

A little time passed and then, one fine autumn day as the soldier was hunting in the forest, he met the two villains who had stolen his money. They had been kicked out of the army because they were idle, and no one would give them a job, and so they were living rough in the wild woods, keeping themselves alive on berries and nettle soup.

The two villains did not recognize the soldier because he was dressed in such fine clothes and was riding a magnificent horse. But the soldier recognized them! Yes, and as he looked down on them he thought that he would have them taken to the gallows and hanged until they were dead. But as he looked at them in their rags and tatters, and with their bare, scratched feet, he felt pity in his heart.

Ah, he thought. God was merciful to me, so must I be merciful to these wretches.

So the soldier forgave the villains and he fed them and clothed them and told them who he was. The two wretches were amazed, but he said:

'Ah, when you left me for dead under the gallows-tree God did not forget his servant. No, he sent three carrion crows and I heard the secrets of Heaven and Earth and now I am married to the King's daughter and I am a prince. I live in my own palace and I have fine clothes and a fine horse, and I have servants and soldiers who do my every bidding. So does the merciful God bring forth good from evil.'

The two villains knelt before the soldier and thanked him and said that they were sorry for the evil they had done him. That is what they said, but their dark hearts were bitter and envious. That very evening, as dusk drew near, one of the villains said:

'Why should that soldier have all the good fortune? Let us go to the gallows and hear what the crows say. Then we, too, will be rich and powerful.'

'Aye,' said the other villain. 'Let us do that. And when we are rich and powerful then we will have that soldier murdered!'

And the first villain agreed! Their hearts were as twisted as old hawthorns.

The sun went to his bed of fire and, as the moths came out, the two villains went to the gallows and lay beneath it. But they did not think of the Saviour of the world, nor did they repent their sins. Instead they got drunk and fell asleep.

The birds of the forest ceased singing and, at the wolf hour, the three carrion crows came from the fields and perched upon the gibbet. They croaked and krurked and looked around with their sharp eyes, and then the first crow spoke.

'Krah!' it called. 'Krah! Sisters, I have flown many a mile today and I have heard many things and I have seen many things and, sisters, listen! Someone has found the well in the town and now there is water for all the humans!'

The other two crows croaked angrily and jabbed their sharp beaks into the air.

'Krah!' called the crow. 'Listen. The old King's daughter is cured! Someone has found the toad which lived in the mill-pond and given it to the Princess in a broth.'

The crows were even angrier. They clicked their beaks and spread their wings.

'Krah!' the crow said. 'And worst of all, my sisters, the blind can see!'

The crows called and croaked and their scaly claws scraped on the gallows beam.

'Someone has been spying on us,' said the crow. 'Some human has crept upon us and heard our secrets and now men know what we know. If I could find him, why, I would—' Just then one of the two villains rolled on to his back and gave a huge, drunken snore.

The crows heard him. They swung their beaks around like daggers and they stared down and saw the villains.

'There are the spies,' they called. 'There are the spies who have stolen from us the secrets of Heaven and Earth!'

They fluttered down from the gallows and buffeted the

villains in the face with their strong, black wings; and they pecked out the villains' eyes so that the wretches were blinded and killed.

The next day the Soldier-Prince came riding past on his fine horse and found their bodies; and from the goodness and mercy of his heart he ordered that they should be buried. And buried they were, underneath the gallows of the carrion crows, and there they lie in their graves until this day.

And so, according to his word, God ensures that to him who does evil, evil is done, and that to him who does good, good is done in return.

The Brave Little Tailor or Seven at One Blow

Near the famous town of Hamelin, where the Pied Piper killed the rats and stole away the children there lived a tailor. He was only a little fellow but he was cheerful and easy-going and, as he sat in his window, stitching away and whistling like a lark, he made the whole street seem brighter.

One fine summer day he was at his work when a farmer's wife came down the street selling home-made jam.

'Ah,' said the tailor. 'Jam! That will make life sweeter.'

He called to the woman who lugged her heavy basket up the stairs and laid out her jars on the table. The tailor went through the pots as if the fate of the world depended on his choice. He looked at them all, and smelt them all, yes, and he tasted them all for free. He was no fool, you know.

In the end he picked up a pot of plum jam and said that he liked that the best. After all her work the woman

69

expected him to buy at least five pounds' worth, but the tailor said, 'Give me four ounces, my dear, and if that comes to a quarter of a pound I shan't argue with you.'

The woman doled out four ounces. 'Don't eat it all at once,' she said in a sarcastic way, and flounced out.

The little tailor rubbed his hands together and smacked his lips. 'Now,' he cried, 'may God bless this jam and may it bring me health and strength.'

He went to his cupboard, took out a loaf of black bread, cut a slice, and spread the jam on it.

'Ah ha!' he said. 'This won't taste bitter,' and he smacked his lips again because he was a man who liked life. Still, he thought, I'll just finish this jacket before I eat.

He laid aside the bread and dashed at the jacket, sewing like a madman, sticking in huge stitches which got bigger and bigger, because he was so anxious to finish and have his bread and jam.

It was a warm day and while the tailor was stitching a fly buzzed through the window and landed on the jam. A second later another fly flew in, then another, and another, then ten, then twenty, then hundreds and hundreds, all hovering over the bread and jam like a black cloud.

The tailor heard the buzzing of the flies and turned around. 'Hey!' he shouted. 'Who asked you to come in? Get out. Get out at once. Do you hear me?'

However, the flies could not speak German and they kept coming in through the window like an enormous air force. At last the tailor lost his temper. 'All right, then,' he cried. 'If you won't listen to reason then I'll give you what for.'

He picked up a fly swat and lashed out at the flies,

and when he lifted the swat he saw no fewer than SEVEN dead flies lying on their backs with their legs in the air.

'Good heavens,' said the tailor. 'Seven dead flies! Seven! And in one go!' He looked at himself in his mirror and swelled his chest. 'My word,' he said. 'So that is the sort of fellow you are. Seven at one blow. The whole town will hear of this.'

He sat down on his bench, took a vest, and embroidered it with large letters, like a T-shirt:

SEVEN AT ONE BLOW!

The tailor put on the vest and admired himself in the mirror. 'Little but good,' he said. 'Yes indeed. SEVEN! Did I say that the town will hear of this? Why, the whole *world* will know of it,' and his heart fluttered with joy and pride like a lamb's tail.

The tailor locked his little shop but before he left he looked about to see if there was anything useful he could take with him. He found a piece of ripe cheese which he put in one pocket and in his other pocket he put his tame canary. Then he set out to seek his fortune in the wide world.

His way led over the mountains but the little tailor had a spring in his step and he tripped along as lightly as a deer. Up hill and down dale he went, whistling 'Sweet Nightingale', and without a care in the world.

The hills grew bigger and steeper and wilder, and before long the tailor had left the world of men and was in a land where anything could happen, and often did, as the tailor soon found out: for, turning a corner, he found, lying across the road and looking peacefully about him, an enormous giant.

However, the little tailor was not afraid. He walked straight up to the giant and poked him in the big toe.

'Good morning, friend,' he called. 'Having a bit of a rest, are you? Just lying there looking at the view? Well, I am off into the world to try my luck. Why not come along with me?'

The giant looked down on the tailor. 'What?' he rumbled. 'Go with you? Why, you miserable little insect, I could blow you into eternity with one puff. Be off with you.'

'Oh?' The tailor stepped back a pace. 'Just hold on there, you old church-tower. Just you watch out who you are talking to. I'll show you what kind of man I am.' He opened his coat. 'Take a look at my chest. Go on.'

The giant peered down and saw the words on the tailor's vest:

SEVEN AT ONE BLOW!

Oh, the giant thought. Seven at one blow. There is more to this little shrimp than meets the eye, for he thought that the seven were seven men, not seven flies. 'Still,' he said to himself, 'I will give this pygmy a test.' He picked up a rock and squeezed it until it ground into powder. 'How about that?' he growled.

The little tailor smiled. 'Child's play. Watch this.' He took out the piece of ripe cheese from his pocket and squeezed it until the juice ran from it. 'See that,' he said. 'Water from a rock. Can you do that?'

The giant could hardly believe his eyes but he did not want to be beaten by a little chap who did not reach up to his knee. He picked up another stone and hurled it into the air. Up went the stone, up and up, and then it soared back and landed across the valley, about half a mile away.

'See if you can beat that,' said the giant.

The little tailor scratched his nose. 'Not bad,' he said. 'But it came back down to earth, didn't it? I will throw a stone so high that it will never come back to earth.'

He took his canary from his other pocket and threw it upwards. The bird was so glad to have its freedom that it soared into the air and did not return.

'There,' said the tailor. 'How is that for a throw?'

The giant rubbed his eyes but he could not deny what he had just seen. 'You are a good thrower,' he said. 'Yes, I'll give you that. But throwing stones is neither here nor there. Let's see what you are really made of. Come on, follow me.'

The giant led the way to a wood where a huge oak tree, which had been struck by lightning, was lying on the ground.

'Right,' he said. 'If you are as strong as you think you are, help me to carry this tree.'

'Nothing to it,' said the tailor. 'You take the bole and I will take the branches, which are the heaviest part of the tree. Lead the way, old cloud-scraper.'

The giant heaved the bole of the tree on to his shoulders and staggered off. With the huge trunk on his shoulders he could not see what was happening behind him and so the tailor sat on a bough and, as the giant dragged the tree along he swung his legs and whistled the famous tune: 'Three Tailors Rode Out of The City Gate, All on A Fine May Morning'.

The giant lurched down the mountainside, panting for breath, and with his face getting redder and redder. At last he could go no further. 'Look out,' he shouted, 'I'm going to let go.'

The tree crashed to the ground but the tailor leaped

nimbly from the bough and when the giant turned around he saw the little man holding up a branch and looking as cool as a cucumber.

The tailor shook his head. 'Goodness,' he said. 'Don't say that you are tired already.'

The giant wiped his forehead. 'I don't know how you do it,' he panted. 'There is something going on here I don't understand. Still, now we have started we might as well go on together.'

The two of them walked on down the mountainside. After a little while they came to a cherry tree. The giant reached up to the top of the tree, where the ripest fruits grow, and pulled a branch down. 'Here you are,' he said. 'Hold on to this and pluck yourself some cherries.'

The tailor took hold of the branch but of course he could not hold it down and it sprang back and took him with it. He flew through the air and landed on the other side of the tree. The giant looked up from where he was sitting eating cherries and scowled.

'What's this?' he bellowed. 'Aren't you strong enough to hold down a little branch?'

The tailor smiled. 'Of course I'm strong enough,' he said. 'Do you think that a man who has killed SEVEN at one blow can't hold down a cherry branch. I just jumped over the tree for a bit of exercise. See if you can do it.'

The giant did not want to be beaten again so he stepped back, rushed forward, and gave a big leap. But the tree was too tall for him and he ended up sitting in the branches like an idiot. He climbed down and pulled twigs and cherries from his beard.

'All right,' he said. 'You are the best man. Come and spend the night with me in my house.'

The tailor followed the giant into a valley and in the

evening they came to a vast, gloomy cave with a fire roaring away in the middle of it. By the fire there was another giant eating a whole roast lamb which he held as if it was no more than a chop. The giant gave the tailor a piece of meat which was tiny to *him*, although it would have fed the little man for a whole week. However, the tailor took it and sat by the fire.

Ah, he thought, this is seeing the world, right enough. Who would have guessed that the world held such wonders, or that I would see them?

When he had eaten, the first giant showed him a bed and the tailor climbed into it. However, the bed was too big and the blankets, made for a giant, were so heavy that they almost crushed him, so he slipped out of the bed and curled up in a corner.

Lucky for the tailor! For when midnight came, the first giant, who was mad with jealousy, picked up a huge iron bar, jumped at the bed, and smashed it so hard that the bar went clean through it.

At the crack of dawn the giants left the cave. It was much later when the tailor woke up. He had some porridge, cleaned his teeth, then went out.

Before long he came across the giants who were picking berries in the woods. When they saw the jaunty figure of the little tailor they were terrified that he had come to kill them in revenge and they screamed and ran away as fast as their legs could carry them!

'What on earth is the matter?' wondered the tailor. He ran after the giants but that only frightened them more and they ran away faster and hid in the forest.

The tailor shrugged and ambled off, wandering here and there, just as his fancy took him. After a few hours he came to a palace. As he was tired he lay down in the garden and went to sleep. While he lay on the grass the courtiers came from the palace to look at him and they saw on his vest:

SEVEN AT ONE BLOW!

'My word,' they said. 'Who is this hero who has come amongst us? See, he has killed seven at one blow! We must tell the King.'

They ran off and told the King and he sent for the tailor. 'Now then,' he said. 'I see by your vest that you are a mighty hero. Will you join my army?'

'Oh, yes,' said the tailor. 'I'll do that. In fact that is why I came here. Just show me your enemies and I will deal with them. Look—' and he pointed to his vest:

SEVEN AT ONE BLOW!

The King was very pleased to have such a brave man in his army and he made the tailor a general on the spot and gave him a fine house.

The tailor was happy, too. 'This is all right,' he said. 'I *am* doing well for myself. Only the other day I was just a tailor and now I am a general. This is what you call seeing the world.'

However, the King's other generals were not at all happy. 'If we have a war,' they said, 'this man will kill seven with every blow he strikes and there will be nothing left for us to do, and the King will sack us. We must get rid of him.'

Together they went to the King and said that they would leave his service unless the tailor was sacked. The King scratched his head. He certainly did not want to lose his faithful soldiers for the sake of the tailor, on the other hand he was afraid that if he did sack the little man then the tailor would declare war against him. For a long time he wondered what to do and then he had an idea. He sent for the tailor and said this:

'Now then, I wonder if you will do me a favour?'

'Certainly, your Majesty,' the tailor said. 'Anything at all. Just go ahead, and don't be afraid to ask.'

The King felt like jumping off his throne and kicking the tailor right out of the palace but he swallowed his annoyance.

'Thank you,' he said. 'The thing is this. In the Great Forest there are two giants. They are terrible types. They keep coming out of the forest and robbing and vandalizing my Kingdom. Now, if you will go and kill them, you can marry my daughter, the Princess, and I will give you half my Kingdom. How about that?'

The tailor held up his hand. 'Say no more, your Majesty. I know those giants. I will deal with them for you.'

'Thank you,' said the King. 'Now, I will send a hundred knights with you.'

The tailor laughed. 'Excuse me,' he said, 'but that is not necessary. No, I don't need any help just to deal with two giants.' He pointed to his vest.

SEVEN AT ONE BLOW!

'No,' he went on. 'Just leave it to me. I'll get off right away and you can go and see the vicar about the wedding.'

The tailor set off whistling his favourite tune. He went to the Great Forest and plunged into it. Before long he

77

heard a terrible groaning noise. He peeped around a boulder and saw the two giants lying asleep under a tree, and snoring so loudly that the forest was shaking as if a tempest was raging through it.

The tailor filled his pockets with stones, climbed up the tree, and sat astride a bough. He leaned forward and threw a stone at the first giant. Pank! it went, right on the giant's nose. Then the tailor threw another stone. Pank! that went, too.

The giant turned in his sleep and mumbled some bad words and brushed his nose. Pank! Pank! Pank! the tailor threw down more stones until, finally, the giant woke up in a terrible rage. He glared around with his savage, red eyes, then kicked the other giant.

'Why are you hitting me on the head?' he roared.

'Hitting you?' the other giant rubbed his eyes. 'What are you talking about? You are having a nightmare. Go back to sleep.'

The first giant grumbled but dozed off again. Then the tailor threw stones at the second giant. Pink! Pink! Pink! The stones bounced off the giant's bald head until he woke up. He kicked the first giant:

'Yargh!' he bellowed. 'What are you hitting me for?'

'Ah, shut up,' the first giant cried. 'Now *you* are having a nightmare. Go back to sleep. Go on.'

Both the giants lay down and slept and the tailor threw stones at the first giant again until he woke up again.

'That's enough,' he roared, so loudly that the tree-tops waved. In a rage he jumped upon the second giant. The two giants had a terrible fight, kicking and clawing each other and pulling each other's beards. In the end they pulled up huge trees and beat each other so severely that they both fell down dead.

The tailor climbed down from his tree, took out his sword, and made a cut on each of the giants' chests. Then he went back to the King.

'I've killed them,' he said. 'Both of them, stone dead. Mind you, it wasn't easy. They put up a real fight. In fact they pulled up trees and tried to squash me. But they didn't really have a chance. After all—'

He pulled his coat open and pointed to his vest:

SEVEN AT ONE BLOW!

'It stands to reason,' he said. 'What chance have two against me.'

The King could hardly believe his eyes. 'And you are not hurt at all?'

'No, no, of course not.' The tailor whipped out his sword, did a quick shuffle, and stabbed a cushion. 'It was just like that.'

'All right, all right,' said the King. 'Be careful, don't smash the palace to pieces. That cushion was a present.'

The King sent his knights into the forest to see if the tailor had told the truth and they came back and said that the two giants were certainly dead.

'There you are,' said the tailor. 'Now, about the wedding. Is it all fixed up?'

The King pulled a face because he did not want his daughter to marry such a little fellow, and he definitely did not want to give away half his Kingdom. Besides, the tailor was getting on his nerves. He leaned back in his throne and coughed.

'Well, you see,' he said, 'it is like this. Er . . . in the half of the Kingdom you are going to have there is a savage unicorn. It is as big as an elephant and it is doing a lot of damage, charging about all over the place and goring people. Well, I don't want my daughter to live in a place like that so before you can marry her you will have to catch the unicorn—'

'Kill it,' cried the tailor.

'No,' said the King. 'When I say catch it, I mean catch it. It is unlucky to kill unicorns. No, you must catch it and bring it back alive.'

The King leaned back and smiled. That will fix you, he thought.

But the tailor was as chirpy as ever. 'Right,' he said. 'Savage unicorn, catch him, bring him back alive, get married. No problem. No problem at all. After all—'

He began to open his coat but the King waved his hand, testily.

'Yes, I know, I know, seven at one blow. Just get the unicorn, that's all.'

The tailor tripped away and that night when he was in bed the King said to the Queen. 'I really hope that little man gets squashed by the unicorn. I really hope so.'

The next day the tailor took a rope and a saw and went into the West Kingdom. Before long the unicorn had scented him and it came charging through the forest like an express train. The tailor stood with his back against an oak tree. At the last second, just when it seemed that the unicorn's terrible horn would skewer him, he jumped into the air, caught hold of a branch, and swung upwards, like an acrobat. The unicorn could not stop itself and drove its horn deeply into the tree. And because a unicorn's horn is twisted like a corkscrew it could not pull it out again.

The tailor climbed down the tree, tied the rope around the unicorn's neck, sawed off its horn, and led it back to the King.

The King almost fainted when he saw the tailor return. Oh, my word, he thought. What can I do now? Then he had another idea.

'Listen,' he said. 'I have decided not to give you the West Kingdom, but the East Kingdom. That is the best half. The trouble is that there is a wild boar running mad, there. If you can kill the boar then you can get married.'

'No problem, your Majesty,' the tailor cried. 'Leave it to me,' and before the King could stop him he had opened his coat and pointed to his vest and

SEVEN AT ONE BLOW!

After his breakfast the tailor set out to hunt the wild boar. The King sent his huntsmen along with him but the tailor told them to wait at the edge of the forest, and they were not sorry, either. The boar had already killed a dozen huntsmen.

The tailor went into the forest and before long the boar came rushing at him with its mouth gaping and its tusks dripping. The tailor ran off as fast as his legs could carry him until he came to a chapel. He ran inside and the boar ran after him. However, the tailor jumped through the window. The boar tried to follow him but it was too big to get through and before it could turn around the tailor had dashed back around the chapel and slammed the door shut. The tailor went for the huntsmen and by the time they had got to the chapel the boar was dead because it had eaten a pile of dusty hymn books and choked to death.

The huntsmen took the dead boar back to the King and when the King saw it he screamed. But there was nothing he could do about it, and he could not think of another excuse for putting off the wedding, and so the tailor married the Princess and had half the Kingdom—and the best half at that.

The tailor was very happy. Talk about seeing the world, he thought. What a lucky day for me when I bought the jam and then killed SEVEN at one blow.

A few months went by and then, one night, the new Queen heard the tailor talking in his sleep.

'Two pairs of trousers and a waistcoat,' he was saying. 'Yes, sir, I can make those. Yes, sir, call again in a week. Cheapest tailor in the town, sir.'

The Queen was horrified and she ran and told her father and he was horrified, too.

'My God!' he shouted. 'A tailor! A tailor! My daughter married to a tailor! I shall be the joke of the world!' He was a terrible snob, you know. However, he patted his daughter on the hand. 'Never mind, my dear, don't worry. What we will do is this. Tonight, when you go to bed, leave the bedroom door open. At midnight when that . . . that . . . that terrible man is asleep, I will send ten—no—fifty soldiers. They will take him prisoner and put him on a ship that is sailing to the other side of the world and we will never see him again. My God, a tailor!' And he burst into tears.

But listening to the King and his daughter was a servant lad whose father had been a hand-weaver, and to whom the tailor had been kind. He ran to the tailor and told him of the plot.

'Thank you,' said the tailor, 'but don't worry, I can deal with anything. Remember—' and he opened his coat and there were the words:

SEVEN AT ONE BLOW!

That night the tailor went to bed but, although he closed his eyes he stayed awake. When midnight struck he snored, and pretended to talk in his sleep.

'Aha!' he shouted, 'Oho! Yes, sir, two pairs of trousers and a waistcoat. Yes sir, ready in one week. I have killed two giants, I have captured a unicorn as big as an elephant, I have killed the wild boar, and I slew

SEVEN AT ONE BLOW!

I am not afraid of anything in the whole wide world. Why should I be afraid of those men who are standing outside my bedroom door?'

The soldiers heard the tailor shout and they were so afraid that they ran away as if the Devil himself was at their heels.

From then on not one person dared to say anything against the brave little tailor and he remained king and ruled his people wisely and well. The poor servant lad he made a duke and his father an earl. And over his palace, in letters of gold, the tailor had written:

SEVEN AT ONE BLOW!

The Grave Mound

O ne day a rich farmer stood in his farmyard looking at his fields and garden. He was pleased with what he saw. His corn was thick and strong and gleamed golden in the sun, and his orchards were heavy with fruit. He walked past his barn, which was bursting with grain from last year's harvest, and went into his stables. The horses there shone with good health and their coats sparkled like cut glass. In the byre were well fed oxen and cows, and the dairy was brim-full of cream.

The farmer walked back to his farmhouse, scattering hens and ducks out of his way, and went into his parlour. From a secret place he took out a huge iron chest and opened it. Inside, it was stacked with gold and silver and five-pound notes.

The farmer rubbed his hands together and smiled a fat smile as he looked at all his possessions. Just then he heard a loud knock, but the knock was not at the door of his parlour, but at the door of his heart.

Aye, the knock was at the door of his heart, for every heart has a door and that door may be open and allow mercy and pity and charity to enter, or, like the farmer's, it may be as tight shut as a prison and not allow envy, pride, and greed to escape.

And so there was a knock at the door of the farmer's heart and a voice spoke to him: 'Farmer,' said the voice, 'you are rich. Everything you desire you have a hundred times over. But what have you done with your riches? Have you cared for your family? Have you been good to the poor? Have you shared your bread with the hungry and your wine with the thirsty? Have you been contented with what you have, or have you desired more, and yet more? Speak!'

Slowly, in a voice as creaky as an old hinge, the heart answered. 'Ah, I have been without mercy or pity. I have been cruel to my own family and if a beggar came to the door I drove him away and set the dogs on him. Never have I thought of God but always considered myself. And if I owned all that the sky covers I still would not have enough.'

When the farmer heard his own heart answer like this he went pale and had to sit down before he fainted.

Just then there came another knock. But this time it was not a knock at his heart but a knock on the parlour door. The farmer called, 'Come in,' and a man entered.

The man was a neighbour of the farmer, a poor man with a large family who scraped a living from a patch of dry land, and who paid half his earnings in rent. He stood before the farmer, his cap in his hand, and licked his lips: 'Farmer,' he said, 'you're not one to give anything away, but I'm like a drowning man who grabs at straws. My family is starving and I have no money. Will you lend me four sacks of flour until the next harvest?'

The farmer looked at the poor man. An hour before he would have kicked him out without thinking twice about it, but since then that voice had spoken from his heart, and now, like a sunbeam, mercy began to melt his icy hardness.

'I know that you think I am a skinflint,' he said, 'and it is true. I have been. But now . . . well, anyway, I will not lend you four sacks of flour, I will *give* you eight. But only on one condition.'

'Hello,' said the poor man to himself. 'Here it comes.' He looked at the floor and said, 'What is the condition?'

'It is this,' said the farmer. 'When I am dead you must watch by my grave for three nights.'

The poor man was unhappy at this but he had to get the flour and so he agreed.

Now it is a strange thing but the farmer might almost have seen the future, because in less than a week he dropped down dead. No one knew why he died, and nobody cared much either, for there was no sorrow over his death. However, when he was buried, the poor man remembered his promise to watch by the grave for three nights. Actually, he would have been glad to forget all about it, but, as he thought: The farmer did well by me. He fed my family when I was desperate and, in any case, I gave my word and so I must keep it.

That night, when everyone had gone to bed, he wrapped up warm, took a thick club, and went to the graveyard and sat by the farmer's grave. It was a silent night. Only an owl screeched in the yew tree and bats fretted the moon. The man dozed the night away and when dawn came, went home.

On the second night the man went to the grave again and again the night passed quietly, but on the third night he felt uneasy and frightened, as if he knew that

86

something was going to happen, although what that might be he could not tell.

For an hour or two he sat by the grave, and this night the owls' calls sounded sinister, as if something other than an owl was calling from the darkness of the night, and the bats which flittered across the moon made the man think of demons and devils.

At eleven o'clock the church bell tolled and the man heard a movement by the church wall. 'Who's there?' he called. 'Who is that?'

There was no answer and the man picked up his club and took a step forward, although he felt more like dashing off the other way as fast as his legs could carry him. Then, from the shadow of the yew tree a man stepped forward. He wore a tall, pointed hat and a huge cape with the collar turned up.

The poor man almost jumped out of his skin when he saw this but he raised his club and said, 'Stay where you are or I will knock your brains out,' although his voice was trembling like an old woman's.

The man in the tall hat laughed, a low, chilling laugh, and took a step nearer, but, before the poor man dropped dead of heart failure, he swung his tall hat off, and, in the moonlight, showed his face. He was not a young man, nor an old man either. His eyes were sharp and his face was hard and marked with scars.

'Who are you?' asked the poor man. 'What are you looking for in this graveyard? Are you not afraid?'

The stranger laughed again. 'I am looking for nothing,' he said, 'and I am afraid of nothing, either. I am like the lad in the story who had to learn how to shudder, only he got the King's daughter and I have always been poor. No, I am nothing but a soldier who has been paid off and I am going to spend the night here because I have no money for a bed in a lodging.'

The poor man was pleased when he heard that. 'If you are without fear then stay with me here and keep watch. I have a feeling that something is going to happen and I am afraid.'

'Well,' said the soldier, 'keeping watch is a soldier's business so I will stay with you. Besides, I think something will happen, too.'

'What do you mean?' asked the poor man.

'Why,' the soldier sat on the ground and wrapped his cloak around himself. 'The owl has stopped screeching and the bats have gone away and, look, a cloud has covered the moon and all the world is in darkness.'

The peasant shivered and sat down next to the soldier and he wasn't sorry that he had a fearless man with him, I can tell you.

An hour went by and the church clock began to toll twelve and, as the last chime was struck, there was a smell of brimstone in the air and a shrill noise, like a cannon-ball whistling through the air, and suddenly the Devil himself dressed in fine clothes and with a red feather in his cap appeared before the two men.

'Aha!' cried the Devil. 'Aha! Ahee! Ahee! Aha! Be off with you both before I drag you down to my fire. The man lying in this grave belongs to me and if you don't clear off I will break your necks for you.'

'Will you now?' said the soldier and he leaned back against a gravestone and lit his pipe. 'Well, you are not my Colonel and I don't have to take orders from you.'

The Devil was taken aback by that. 'Aren't you afraid of me?' he asked.

The soldier laughed. 'It takes more than a whiff of

brimstone and a red feather to frighten me. I don't even know the meaning of the word. Now hop it before I get angry.'

The Devil rubbed his chin. My word, he thought. These are two tough customers and no mistake. The best thing I can do is bribe them to go away. He cleared his throat and began to sing a sweeter song. 'Now look here, lads,' he said. 'I want the soul of that farmer lying there so I'll tell you what I'll do. I'll give you a bag of money if you will clear off.'

'Now you're talking,' the soldier said. 'But one bag of money won't do. If you will bring enough gold to fill my boot, then we'll get out of your way.'

The Devil looked at the soldier's riding boots. 'Mm,' he said. 'I don't have that much money on me but I know a money-lender in the town. He'll lend me that much. I'll go and get it.'

The Devil whizzed away and the soldier took his boot off. 'Now, comrade,' he said to the poor man. 'We'll pull that old charcoal burner's nose for him. Hand me a knife.'

The poor man gave the soldier a knife and he cut the sole from his boot. 'Right,' he said. 'Watch this.' With the knife he dug a deep hole among some long grass by the edge of the grave and put his boot over it. 'That will do,' he said. 'Now let that chimney-sweep come.'

Not long after, the Devil came back with a bag of gold in his hand. The soldier pointed to his boot. 'Just pour it in there, but I'll tell you now, that won't be enough to fill it.'

The Devil shook out the gold and it fell into the boot and through into the hole and the boot stayed empty.

'You stupid old fool,' said the soldier. 'Didn't I tell you that wouldn't be enough? Go and bring some more.'

The Devil scratched his head, but he went back to the money-lender and came back with a bigger bag of gold. That went into the boot, too, and into the hole. The Devil peered into the boot with his burning eyes and saw for himself that the boot was still empty. He shook his head; 'You must have mighty big feet,' he muttered.

'What of it?' cried the soldier. 'Did you think that I had a cloven foot like you? Come on, get more gold.'

The Evil One went off again and this time he came back with a bag so full of gold that he could hardly carry it. Puffing and panting, he poured it into the boot and the gold just fell right through into the hole. This time the Devil was angry.

'Someone is playing a trick,' he roared, and he grabbed the boot to see what was happening. But just at that moment the first ray of the rising sun pierced the darkness of the night and the Devil had to rush off back to his fiery home. The soul of the farmer was saved.

The poor man looked at the heap of gold and he could hardly believe his eyes at how much there was. He wanted to divide the gold half and half, but the soldier said, 'No. Give my half to the poor and I will come and live with you in your cottage. With what is left we can live in peace, as long as it pleases God.'

And it must have pleased the Creator for many a long year, for that is how long they lived together.

Snow White
and Rose Red

A poor widow lived in a solitary glade. In her garden she had two rose-trees, one of which gave red roses and the other white. The widow had two step-daughters. One of the girls had creamy cheeks and so she was called Snow White, and the other girl, who had ruddy cheeks, was called Rose Red.

The two daughters were good girls, as happy and cheerful and industrious as ever two children in the world have been. Snow White was quiet and gentle and liked to stay at home with her mother whereas, like her name, Rose Red was more fiery and active and liked to run in the meadows gathering flowers and watching the birds and the beasts. But different though they were by nature, the girls loved one another, and walked together hand in hand, and they swore that they would never be parted and that whatever the one had, the other would share.

Although the girls lived in a solitary place they were never lonely or bored. The woods and fields were their playground and, even though they often wandered deep in the forest gathering berries, no beast ever harmed them. The merry hare would eat cauliflowers from their hands, the doe danced by their side, the stag bounded with joy when he saw them and the birds did not fly away as they approached but stayed perching on the boughs, singing their secret songs.

Even if the girls stayed so late in the woods that night overtook them they were not afraid. They would lie down on a mossy bank, cover themselves with leaves, and sleep until the morning came and, because their mother knew that they would be safe she did not fret and worry about them.

Snow White and Rose Red kept their mother's cottage as bright as a new pin. In the summer Snow White took care of the house and every morning she placed a garland of roses by her mother's bed. In the winter Rose Red did the housework, lighting the fire and polishing the brass and copper pans so that the reflections of the firelight leaped and flickered on them. Then, in the evening, the mother would put on her spectacles and read the girls their favourite stories: *The Brave Little Tailor*, *The Frog Prince*, and *Sleeping Beauty*, although their favourite of all was *Snow White and the Seven Dwarfs*. And as Mother read aloud, a lamb lay by the fire and a white dove perched on the mantelpiece with its head under its pearly wing. It was a sight to see and, although they were poor, all the riches in the world could not have made them happier.

One winter's night there was a terrible blizzard. The wind howled down the chimney and buffeted the windows and the driving snow smothered all the woods and fields. But inside the cottage it was warm and snug as the little family sat by the fire, and the mother read aloud, the lamb and the dove slept, and the cuckoo clock reminded them that spring would come again.

And then, as the kettle sang and as Rose Red was taking the teapot from the cupboard, there came a terrible hammering at the door. The children looked at their mother with round eyes but she calmly took off her spectacles and put down her book.

'That may be some poor traveller caught in the blizzard,' she said. 'Open the door, Rose Red.'

Rose Red undid the bolts and opened the door. There was a blast of wind and snow and lurching into the parlour came a huge, black bear! Rose Red screamed, the lamb dashed into the kitchen, the dove tried to get into the cupboard, the cuckoo in the cuckoo clock stayed behind his little door, and Snow White hid behind her mother's chair!

The bear wagged his great head and showed his yellow fangs, but as the mother picked up the poker, he grunted:

'Please don't be afraid, and please don't hit me with the poker. I am only a poor bear who is lost in the storm. I am nearly frozen to death and I wonder if I can warm myself by your fire for I will never get to my den tonight.'

'Poor bear,' said the mother. She closed the door and patted the bear on the head. 'Of course you must stay. Lie by the fire and get warm, but be careful you don't scorch your fur. Come, Snow White and Rose Red, the bear won't hurt you.'

The girls came out, and the lamb and the dove, and the cuckoo cuckooed eight o'clock. The bear blew on his paws and lay in the hearth. Icy snow was plastered on his shaggy coat and the children got brooms and knocked it off. The bear blew a great sigh through his nostrils, gave a growl of content, heaved over on to his side, and stretched out his massive paws.

'Thank you, children,' he said. 'And thank you, mother. It isn't everyone who would let a poor bear into their house.'

The mother gave the bear a bowl of milk and some honey. By the time he had finished the children had lost all fear of their hairy guest. A little nervously at first, but then boldly, they began to play with the bear, pulling his shaggy fur, sitting on him, and pulling his tail. The bear put up with it all good-naturedly, and when the girls flicked him with hazel rods he grunted and growled as if they were hurting him, although he did not feel their blows any more than he would have felt a fly walking on his back.

When bedtime came the children kissed the bear goodnight and went to their room. The bear stood up as if he was ready to leave but the mother said:

'You don't have to go, bear. You are welcome to stay the night here by the warm fire.'

The bear thanked her and slept the night in the hearth, but, as soon as day dawned and the children had opened the door, he lumbered off through the snow. The children and the mother were sorry to see the bear go, and without his great black bulk by the fire the house seemed quiet and empty. But that night, as the family sat by the fire, there was a knocking on the door and when Rose Red opened it the bear poked his black head into the room.

'Oh, bear,' said the mother. 'Are you lost again?'

The bear coughed and, although it is not easy for a bear to do so, it looked sheepish. 'Well,' he said, I . . . I'm not *exactly* lost. No, not exactly, but . . . well, to tell you the truth, I liked it so much last night that I thought I would come back. I hope you don't mind.'

'Of course not,' said the mother. 'We are very glad you have come back.'

From that time on the bear came to the cottage every night at eight o'clock and the children played with him as he lay on the hearth and told them many bearish stories.

But, as the cuckoo in the clock had promised, spring came again. The hedges were white with may instead of snow, and the trees were spangled with buds. One day, as the hoopoe, who is called the cuckoo's clerk because he always comes a few days earlier than the cuckoo, showed his yellow crest in the woods, the bear came to the cottage.

'I must go away,' he said. 'I shall be away all summer and you will not see me again until the winter-time.'

The mother and the children were sad. 'Why are you leaving us, dear bear?' they asked.

'Ah,' said the bear, and suddenly he looked fierce and frightening. 'In my den I have many treasures. The wicked dwarfs in the forest want to steal them because they are mad for gold and jewels. They are for ever trying to dig mines in the ground under my den so that they can break in and steal my wealth. In the winter the treasure is safe because the ground is frozen so hard that the dwarfs cannot dig their mines. But now that spring is here and the sun has warmed the earth those wicked little men will be digging for all they are worth. I tell you, they will steal everything they can lay their hands on and once they have hidden the treasure in their caves in the mountains it is not easy to find again, believe me.'

'Well,' said the mother. 'If you must go then you must. But we are very sorry. Very sorry indeed.'

'And I am sorry, too,' said the bear. He gave a big sniffle and turned his head away and wiped a tear which had trickled down his nose. 'Goodbye,' he said and dashed through the door and across the meadow and soon he was lost to sight among the trees of the forest. But the bear had run out so quickly that his furry coat was caught on the bolt and a little tuft was torn off, showing the skin underneath. Snow White saw the skin and just for a moment she thought that it glinted as if it was gold, or golden. She could not be sure of what she saw, and it might have been the sun shining on the skin, but it made her thoughtful.

A little time passed and the woods were full of singing birds when, one day, the mother sent the children into the forest to collect mushrooms.

The girls left the house but before they had gone very far they saw a very odd sight. A tree which had been struck by lightning was lying in a field and something was bobbing up and down on it. The children could not imagine what it was, but when they drew near they saw a dwarf with a wrinkled face and a white beard a yard long. The end of the beard was jammed in a cleft in the tree. The dwarf could not free himself although he was jumping about like a dog at the end of a chain.

The dwarf glared at the girls with his fiery red eyes and shook his fist.

'Don't just stand there,' he shouted. 'Come and help me.'

'What is the matter, little man?' asked Rose Red.

'What is the matter? What is the matter?' shouted the dwarf. 'You stupid, staring goose, you can see what is the matter. I came here to cut a little wood for my fire—only a little because we do not need huge blazing fires to cook our scraps of food. We are not like you great big clumsy creatures who need half a forest just to cook your supper. Anyway, as I was cutting my wood my beard caught in this crack and I cannot get it loose and all that you two stupid whey-faced creatures can do is laugh. Help me!'

Snow White and Rose Red did all that they could to free the dwarf. They held him by the head and the neck and pulled and heaved, while the dwarf groaned and moaned, but they could not get him free. At last Rose Red said that she would go and get help.

'You crack-pot,' shrieked the dwarf. 'You have less brains than a sheep. What is the good of getting more people? You two are two too many as it is. Can't you think of anything better to do than pulling my head off?'

Snow White was cross when she heard the dwarf speak to her sister like that. 'Very well, dwarf,' she said. 'If you want to be made free, then free you will be made,' and she pulled out her sewing scissors and snipped off the end of the dwarf's beard.

The dwarf fell on his behind with a bump, jumped to his feet, snatched up a bag of gold which was hidden in the roots of the tree and without even thanking the girls he marched off. Just once he turned around and shook his fist. 'Stupid girls,' he shouted, 'cutting off a piece of my fine beard. I hope you both get the plague.'

The summer came and one fine day Rose Red and Snow White went fishing for their supper. By the river they saw something hopping on the bank like a huge grasshopper. When they got nearer they saw that it was the dwarf again.

'Be careful,' cried Snow White. 'You will fall into the water.'

The dwarf glowered at them. 'It's you two boneheads is it? Trust my luck. Can't you see what is happening? I have been fishing and a big pike has got the hook and the other end of the line is tangled in my beard. The pike is dragging me into the river and I will be drowned. Help me!'

The girls held the dwarf fast but the fishing line was so entangled in his beard that they could not release it. So Snow White took out her scissors and snipped a little more beard off. But was the dwarf grateful that he had been saved from drowning? Not at all. He screeched with rage and stamped his foot.

'You donkey,' he roared. 'First you cut off a quarter of my beard, then you cut off half of it! I can't show my face among my own people like this. I wish that you had run the soles off your feet before you found me again. May the Devil have you both!'

And he picked up a bag of pearls which were hidden under a willow tree and ran off, mumbling and muttering, until he vanished behind a boulder.

The glowing days of autumn came. Apples ripened on the boughs and the swifts flew off to Africa. In the local town the September fair was to be held and the mother sent the children to it to buy thread and needles and pins and laces and ribbons. Their way led over a heath which was scattered with boulders. As the girls walked through the rough grasses they heard a strange mewing sound. They looked up and saw a huge eagle, which was pouncing at something behind a boulder. There was a piteous, heart-rending scream, the girls ran forward, and there behind the rock they saw that same dwarf. The eagle had gripped him in its mighty talons and was about to carry him away.

Just as the eagle was rising into the air the girls grabbed the dwarf. Rose Red held what was left of his beard, and Snow White seized his coat. The eagle beat his great wings but for all his strength and majesty he could not tear the dwarf from the girls' grasp and at last he gave up the struggle and soared away.

The dwarf lay panting on the ground but as soon as he recovered his breath he jumped up in a terrible rage.

'You two geese again!' he bellowed. 'Why is it always you two? Look what you have done to my fine brown coat. It is full of holes now.'

He rubbed his chin and gave an awful scream. 'Yieee! And you have pulled off the rest of my beard, you meddling creatures. I hope you fall down a well and break your necks!'

And without a word of thanks he picked up a bag full of diamonds and ran away to his hole under the rocks.

The autumn ended and the first icy breath of winter came from the north. Snow White and Rose Red went to collect sticks for the fire. They went into a wood and there, in a secret glade, once again they came across the dwarf who was sitting on the ground gloating over his treasure, which he had spread out upon the ground.

The sun slanted through the trees and shone upon the treasure, gold and pearls and diamonds. The gold glowed like the sun itself, the pearls gleamed like the face of the moon, and the diamonds shimmered and sparkled like a rainbow. The girls were enchanted by the sight and stood silently, their breath taken away by the beauty on the grass. But from the corner of his eye the dwarf saw them.

He jumped and his face went as red and dusky as copper with rage. 'Again!' he shouted. 'Again! I am haunted by you two little horrors. What are you gaping at? Why, I ought to . . . ' He lifted up his pickaxe and swung it in the air.

The girls were frightened because they really thought the dwarf would attack them, but as the dwarf cursed and threatened, there was a tremendous bellow from the woods, and the crashing and breaking of twigs and branches, and from the darkness of the trees there came rushing the great black bear!

The bear reared up on his hind legs. Froth swung from his tusks and his eyes were redder than the dwarf's. The little man screamed again, but with fear this time.

'Spare me, bear,' he cried. 'Don't kill me. Look, I will give you all my gold and pearls and diamonds.'

The bear growled, a thick, throbbing growl, which came from the depth of his great chest. The dwarf darted behind the two girls.

'Don't eat me,' he squeaked. 'Why, I am so small that you would not even taste me as I slipped down your throat. And I am as gristly as an old hen. Uuugh! You wouldn't like me at all. But here are two wicked girls who deserve eating, and they are as sweet and tender as young quails. Eat them!'

He pushed the girls forward and tried to run away. But before he could reach his hiding-place the bear cuffed him on the ear and he turned into a hoop and rolled away!

The girls were running away, too, but before they had crossed the glade they heard a voice calling them.

'Snow White,' the voice called. 'Rose Red, do not be afraid. I shan't hurt you.'

They recognized the voice of their friend the bear. But when they turned around they saw that a change was taking place in him. His long muzzle was shrinking, and his fearful claws, and, even as they watched, the bearskin slipped from his shoulders and there stood a fine young man dressed in gold. The young man took the girls home and that night, as they sat around the fire, he told them and their mother his story.

'I am the son of a king,' he said. 'Five years ago I punished that dwarf for swearing. In return he put a spell on me and turned me into a bear so that I was forced to live in the wilderness. This year he stole my treasure, as well, but now he has got his reward, and well he deserved it, and the spell has been broken.'

The children clapped their hands with joy but the mother was a little sad.

'I suppose that now you will go back to your palace,' she said, 'and we shall never see you again.'

The Prince stared into the fire and shook his head. 'No,' he murmured, 'no, I don't think I shall. If I go back there I shall live a pampered, idle life, and I have seen in this little cottage how happily one can live in a simple way. So if I may, I shall stay here and give all my treasure to the poor.'

How happy the family were to hear that. They laughed and sang and cheered. The little lamb bounded about the house and the dove hopped up and down on the mantelpiece, and the cuckoo cuckooed so many times he lost his voice.

The young man became an honest woodcutter and married Snow White, and his brother came to live with them and he married Rose Red. They all lived together happily for many years, and for every one of those years the two rose trees bloomed and gave them roses, red and white.

And as for the malevolent dwarf: he is still a hoop and he is still bowling about the face of the earth. The next time you see a hoop, remember, that could be the dwarf so give him an extra whack with your stick. He certainly deserves it.

The Bear and
the King of the Hedges

One fine May morning, when all the world was reborn, a bear woke up from its winter sleep and lumbered off into the forest to look for honey. By an ash tree he met a wolf. The two beasts were old friends and so they went for a stroll together, enjoying the fresh scent of the young pine needles.

As they ambled through the woods the birds of the air were singing to high Heaven, but one called so loudly that the bear stopped.

'Brother Wolf,' he asked, 'what bird is that which calls so loudly?'

'Ah,' said the wolf, 'Brother Bear, that is the wren. He is the King of the Hedges.'

The bear scratched his nose with his long, black claws. 'The King of the Hedges! Brother, I would like to see his palace for I have never seen a king's palace before.'

'Very well,' said the wolf. 'But we must wait until the King has flown to the hedge and shown us where his palace is hidden.'

The two beasts hid behind a holly tree and waited. After a little while the mother wren flew to the hedge with her beak crammed full of worms.

'That is the Queen of the Hedges,' said the wolf.

A little later the father wren flew to the hedge with his beak full of worms, too.

'That is the King of the Hedges,' said the wolf.

The bear wanted to go to the hedge there and then but the wolf clamped on to his tail with his sharp teeth.

'No, Brother,' he said. 'We must wait until the King and the Queen have flown away.'

The bear could hardly wait, but soon the wrens had stuffed their nestlings with worms and had flown away to find more food.

'Ah,' said the bear, 'now I can see the palace.'

He shook the wolf from his tail and shambled to the hedge. He poked his shaggy head through the thorns and was amazed to see five or six fledglings huddled in a tiny nest.

'What?' said the bear. 'Is this a king's palace? Why, I could put it on the end of my nose and not even know it was there!'

He shook his great head, stared down at the fledglings through his red eyes, and burst out laughing. 'And are these scraggy things the King's children?' he said. 'Goodness me, what a crowd of ragamuffins you are. You look like a family of thieves.'

The young wrens were furious. They stretched their scrawny, yellow necks and opened their beaks.

'No, we are not,' they squawked. 'No we are not. We are good little birds and our parents are honourable. You will be sorry for calling us names, bear. Just you wait until we tell our father what you have said. He is the King of the Hedges and you will pay for insulting us.'

The bear and the wolf were afraid when they heard that. They ran off into the forest and hid in their dens while the young wrens crouched in their nest, piping and screeching with rage.

The father wren and the mother wren returned to the nest with their beaks full of food but the children would not eat. No, they would not touch a thing, not even the juiciest caterpillar.

'We won't eat,' they cried. 'Even if we die of hunger we will not touch one thing until you make the bear apologize for calling us thieves and ragamuffins.'

The father wren perked up his little tail and puffed out his feathers.

'Calm yourselves, little ones,' he said. 'I will make the bear eat his words.'

He swallowed the caterpillars himself and flew through the forest to the bear's den. He perched on a bluebell and called into the den.

'Growler,' he called. 'You in there, old Sorehead. You have insulted my children. Come out. I know that you are there. Come out and apologize.'

But the bear crouched at the end of his den and would not come out.

The wren spread its wings. 'Very well,' it piped. 'I declare a bloody war against you!' Then it flew to its nest.

So war was declared against the bear and he called on all the four-footed creatures on earth to help him: oxen, horses, deer, wolves, dogs and cats, and every other animal which trod the ground.

And the wren called on all its allies, every creature

which flew through the air; and not only birds but insects, too: midges, bees, hornets and flies, they all answered the wren's summons.

The two armies gathered and the time for war had come. The wren sent out spies and the gnat, which was the smallest and craftiest of the insects, flew deep into the forest and found all the animals of the earth gathered in a glade. They were all there: the wolves with their long yellow teeth, stags and oxen with their heavy horns, even the cats with their sharp claws were there. The gnat hid under an oak leaf and spied on them and he saw the bear stand up and he heard the bear speak.

'Animals and friends,' said the bear. 'We have a fine army but we must have a general to lead us into battle. Where is the fox?'

The fox slid forward and sat before the bear.

'Fox,' the bear said, 'you are the most cunning animal in the forest. You must be our General.'

The animals agreed with this. They roared and grunted and mooed and bleated and howled and miaowed their agreement.

'Good,' said the bear. 'Now, fox, we must have a banner to lead us. What shall it be?'

The fox scratched his hind leg and then looked up through his clever eyes.

'I know,' it said. 'See. I have a beautiful, long, red tail. It is so beautiful that it looks like a plume of red feathers. That will be our flag. When we go into battle, if I think that we are winning then I will hold my tail up, like this—' and he waved his tail on high and it did indeed look like a plume of red feathers.

'So,' the fox wagged his head. 'That is good. But if we are losing then I will hold my tail between my legs. Then we must all run away as fast as we can, otherwise we might all be killed by the birds. Is that understood?'

All the animals understood, and the gnat understood, too. It buzzed back through the forest and told the wren everything it had heard.

'Good,' said the wren. 'You have done well, gnat.' And he made the insect a corporal there and then.

The morning came and, as the sun peeped over the rim of the world, deep in the forest a donkey brayed, and at its signal the animals came charging from the trees. Their hooves thundered so that they made the earth quake and the seas shiver!

And where the birds of the air were gathered, a cock crowed, and at its signal the wren with all his army came flying through the air. They screeched and whistled and hooted and screamed, and their wings beating made such a roar that it made the sky shake and the clouds quiver!

The Earth and the Heavens were afraid; but the wren was clever. He knew what he was doing. He called to a hornet and said:

'Hornet, go to the fox and sting him under the tail. He will drop his tail and the animals will think that they have lost the battle and they will all run away.'

As quick as lightning the hornet zoomed away and found the fox and stung him with its long sting. The fox yelped and lifted one leg, but still he kept his tail up and the beasts charged onwards.

The hornet stung the fox again. Tears came into the fox's eyes but he gritted his teeth and kept his tail up, and still the beasts charged forwards.

The hornet took a deep breath. 'Right,' it said. 'This time.' And it waggled its sting and drove it into the fox with all its might and main.

The sting was like a red hot needle and the fox could bear it no longer. Tears ran from his eyes and he yipped with pain and clamped his tail between his legs. The animals saw the tail come down and they thought that the battle was lost and they ran away and hid themselves, each in its den, or burrow, or stable, or pen.

Then the birds saw that they had won the great war against the animals, and they were glad and whistled and chirruped and crowed to their hearts' content.

Crowned with glory the wren and his wife crammed their beaks with caterpillars and worms and flew back to their nest in the hedge. The wren looked fondly on his children.

'Now little ones,' he called, 'eat and be happy for we have won the war against the animals.'

But the young wrens still would not eat! They nestled down and closed their eyes.

'We will not eat,' they piped. 'No, we will eat nothing at all until the bear has come and said that we are fine little birds and true Princes and Princesses.'

'Yes,' said the wren's wife. 'That is quite right. Go at once and bring the bear here and make him apologize.'

The wren flew through the forest and perched on the bluebell.

'Bear,' he called, 'old Growler, come out of there at once.'

The bear came out of his den looking very frightened and the wren sat in the bear's ear.

'Now,' it chirruped. 'You must come back to my palace and see my children and beg their pardon for what you called them. If you do not—why, I will have you pecked to death by my army.'

And just to prove his point he gave the bear's ear a good peck himself!

The bear nodded his head sadly and went to the wren's nest and apologized with tears in his eyes. Then the young wrens squeaked with happiness and ate and drank until the night came, when all birds sleep, except the ghostly owls.

Then the bear crept back to his den, his head hanging down with sorrow.

But all the same, he still thought that the young wrens were a pack of ragamuffins!

The Poor Miller's-Lad
and the Cat Princess

There was an old miller who had neither a wife nor children. What he did have was a fine mill by a stream and three apprentices: Karl, Johann, and Hans.

Karl and Johann thought that they were clever lads. Hans did not think that he was clever at all, but he had a kind heart. The miller kept three cats because of the mice in the mill and Hans was always good to the cats and every night he gave them a bowl of his own milk.

One night, when they were having a supper of roast pike from the stream, the old miller said to his apprentices, 'Lads, I'm getting on a bit and I won't live for ever. I have neither wife nor children so I am going to make my will and leave the mill to one of you. But which one? That's the question.'

The three apprentices looked at each other sidewards. Yes, they thought, yes, that is the question, right enough.

The miller had a glass of beer and wiped his mouth. 'Now then, you have all been good apprentices and so it is hard for me to decide which of you should have the mill. So what I'm going to do is this. Listen.'

The apprentices certainly listened. In fact they listened so hard that their ears waggled!

'Good,' said the miller. 'Now then, I am going to send you three out into the wide world and each of you has to bring me back a horse. Whichever one brings back the best horse can have the mill. How does that suit you?'

Well, it suited Karl. He thought that he was so clever that he would easily bring back the best horse.

It suited Johann, too. He thought that he was so clever that he was sure that he would bring back the best horse.

As for Hans, he merely smiled and gave the cats some of his fish.

The next day the three lads said goodbye to the miller and set off into the wide world. At noon they came to a village and went into an inn to have some bread and cheese. When they had eaten, Karl turned to Hans.

'We are off now,' he said, 'off into the wide world. You might as well stay here and get a job washing dishes. You are so stupid that you could not find a fine horse if you spent the rest of your life looking for one.'

But Hans only smiled and bought some milk for a kitten which was miaowing on the counter.

Karl and Johann left the inn and walked up the village street and Hans followed them, and when the two clever lads left the village and went into the woods, Hans followed them there, also, and every time Karl and Johann turned around they saw Hans walking behind them with a smile on his face.

When night fell, the apprentices were still in the woods

and they began to look for somewhere to sleep, but it was Hans, who was not clever, who found a dry cave.

'This will do us fine,' he said and went in and lay down. The other two lads followed him but they only pretended to go to sleep. Soon Karl nudged Johann in the ribs.

'Come on,' he whispered, 'let's clear off. We don't want Hans traipsing along behind us and gawping at us everywhere we go.'

Johann agreed and those two crafty lads tiptoed out of the cave and ran off through the moonlit fields. They thought that they had done a clever thing, but we shall see what good it did them!

The night passed away, the sun came up, the birds began to sing, and Hans woke up. When he opened his eyes he could hardly believe what he saw. He was in a deep cleft, so deep that he could only just see the sky! It was like being in the deepest well in the world.

'Where am I?' cried Hans. 'What has happened?' but the only reply was his own voice echoing from the walls of the cleft.

Hans was frightened but he pulled himself together. Perhaps I can climb out, he thought. At any rate, if I don't then I shall starve to death down here.

So Hans began to climb out of the cleft. It was a hard climb and twice he slipped and almost dashed himself to death. But in the end he reached the top, hooked his fingers over a ledge, and with a last heave he hauled himself from the cleft and found himself in a dark and tangled forest.

Ah, thought Hans. What will become of me now? I am lost in this dark forest and I am alone in the world. I will never find a fine horse now. In fact I will be lucky if I stay alive.

But sitting and crying never brought home the milk, so Hans set out into the forest. After a while he found a path and he followed it hoping to find a cottage. The path wound through the trees but it did not lead to a cottage. Instead the forest got wilder and more tangled and thicker and darker and Hans was afraid. 'This is a wild place,' he said. 'It must be full of wolves which will eat me if I do not find shelter by nightfall.'

He hurried on, walking, then trotting, and then running, until he was so tired that he had to stop and rest. He sat down on a fallen tree and closed his eyes. When he opened them he saw, sitting before him, washing its face with its paw, a tabby cat.

The cat opened its green eyes and stared at Hans like a hypnotist. Then it opened its mouth and showed its pink tongue and glinting little teeth.

'Hans,' said the cat. 'Where are you going?'

Hans stared at the cat in amazement. A talking cat! He had never heard of such a thing.

'Ah, Puss,' he said, 'there is nothing you can do to help me.'

The cat looked up and its eyes were like green flames. 'Hans,' it purred, 'I know what is in your heart and I know all your desires. You wish to have a fine horse, the finest horse in the whole wide world. Well, Hans, if you will come with me and be my servant for seven years, I will give you a horse. And if you serve me faithfully and well, I will give you the finest horse that the world has ever known. It will be so fine that the richest king on earth has none finer.'

Well, thought Hans, if cats can talk then this must be a magic forest, and if that is so then perhaps this cat can give me a fine horse. In any case, if I don't go with the cat then I shall certainly be eaten by wolves.

So Hans said, 'Very well, cat. I agree.'

The cat trotted off along the path, its tail held high, and Hans followed her until they came to a house.

'Hans,' miaowed the cat, 'this is my home, and here you must serve me for seven years.'

She led the way into the house where there were three kittens, one white, one brown, and one ginger. There was a dinner laid of milk and mouse-pudding. Hans refused the pudding but had milk and bread. While they ate, the three kittens played for them. The white kitten played a cello, the brown kitten played the violin, and the ginger kitten blew a trumpet so hard that its cheeks blew out and its eyes crossed. When they had finished, the cat asked Hans to dance with her.

'No, no,' said Hans. 'I have never danced with a cat before.'

'Very well,' said the cat, and danced with herself, leaping up and down, and twisting gracefully in the air.

Hans went to bed and the kittens helped him to undress. One took off his shoes, another turned down the bedclothes, and the third blew out the light. The next morning they came again. One tied his shoe-laces, one washed his face, and the third wiped him dry with its tail.

After breakfast the cat told Hans that he would have to cut firewood for the stove and do the gardening, and that they would be his tasks for seven years. However, all his tools were of gold and silver and bronze, and he had good food to eat, and, although the cat liked mouse-pudding, she never made Hans eat any. And in all the years that passed Hans never saw one other human being.

The years passed away like the twinkling of an eye, and then one day, Hans went to the cat.

'Mistress,' he said, 'I have been a good servant for seven years and I have done everything you have told me to do. And if you look you will see that although my tools are made of gold and silver and bronze, they are safe and sound, every one.'

'Yes,' answered the cat. 'You have been a good and faithful servant. But you cannot count very well, Hans. You have only served me for six years and you still have one more year to go. While that is passing you must build me a little summer-house. Build it near a stream where I can have clear water to drink, and build it where there are plenty of mice!'

Hans built the house by a clear stream at the edge of a meadow where there were many field-mice. Then he went back to the cat and told her that he had done as she had ordered. The cat went with him and saw the summer-house.

'Very good, Hans,' she purred. 'That is a good little house. You are a faithful worker. And now the seven years have passed and I will be true to my word, and I will show you what no eyes but mine have ever seen before.'

She waved her tail three times and blinked her green eyes three times. 'Now open my little summer-house.'

Hans opened the door and inside there were thirteen horses. Yes, the thirteen finest horses Hans had ever seen in his life. Their sleek coats shone as if they were made of bronze, and their white teeth shone as if they were made of silver, and their eyes shone as if they were made of gold.

'Now,' mewed the cat. 'These are the finest horses in the wide world and you may have one because you have been my faithful servant for seven years, and because you have always been good to little cats.'

115

The cat gave Hans a glass of milk and offered him a mouse sandwich but, very politely, Hans said, 'No thank you.'

Then the cat said, 'Now go, Hans, and in three days' time I will follow you and bring you the finest horse of these thirteen.'

She waved her tail three times and Hans fell asleep. When he awoke he was in the cave where he had fallen asleep with the two clever apprentices.

Well, he thought. That must have been a dream. But when he looked at his coat it was worn into rags. Why, he thought, that is right, because in all the seven years I worked for the cat she never gave me a new coat. Perhaps it wasn't a dream, after all. Anyway, I suppose that I had better be getting off home. I'll bet that Karl and Johann have got two fine horses. I wonder which has the finest?

He walked back through the woods and fields, and the village where he had eaten bread and cheese. The inn was still there and, sitting inside on the counter was the cat Hans had bought a saucer of milk for, and as he passed the inn the cat ran along the window and miaowed at him.

After a while Hans reached the mill. It was still there and the stream still splashed and drove the mill-wheel. The three cats were still there, too, and as Hans walked up the path they jumped through the window and waved their tails and purred and rubbed their sides against his legs.

Karl and Johann were there, also, and each of them had a horse. But they were not fine horses. Karl's horse was blind and Johann's horse was lame, so they had not done well at all. But all the same, when they saw that

Hans had no horse they sneered at him. 'You always were stupid,' they said, but Hans only smiled.

'My horse will be here in three days' time,' he said. 'It will be the finest horse in the wide world,' he said.

Karl and Johann burst out laughing. 'When you get a horse, cats will talk,' they sneered. Hans did not answer. He just bent down and stroked the cats.

The three lads went into the mill for their dinner, but when the old miller saw how ragged Hans was he would not have him in the house.

'Why,' he growled, 'if any respectable person came in here and saw you sitting at my table in your rags I would be ashamed of myself. Get out.'

So Hans had to eat outside with the horses. And when he tried to go to bed Johann and Karl would not let him into the bedroom and told him to sleep in the hen-house. Again, Hans did not complain or argue. He just smiled and did as he was told, but the three cats sat outside the hen-house to make sure no rats or mice ran over him.

For three nights Hans ate with the horses, and for three nights he slept in the hen-house, and for three nights the cats watched over him.

And then, early on the morning of the fourth day, the cats began running about, and jumping and miaowing, and waving their tails. They were so excited that they would not even drink their morning milk!

The miller and Johann and Karl came out of the mill to see what was going on and, coming up the lane, they saw a coach drawn by twelve horses. What a coach that was! It was made of gold and silver and bronze. And behind the coach was a servant with ginger hair leading the finest horse which had ever been seen in the history of the world. And in the coach was a princess and that

117

princess was the tabby cat for whom Hans had worked for seven long years.

The Princess looked down on the miller. 'Where is the lad called Hans?' she asked.

The miller could hardly believe his ears. 'Hans?' he asked. 'Do you mean Hans? Does a fine princess like you want to speak to Hans?'

'Are you deaf?' asked the Princess. 'Yes, Hans! Hans! Hans! Where is he?'

'Why,' the miller said, 'he is so ragged that he lives in the hen-house.'

The Princess frowned. 'Faithful Hans in a hen-house? Bring him to me at once.'

Hans was brought to the Princess and her servants took him to the river and bathed him and dressed him in fine clothes so that he looked like a prince. Then the Princess demanded to see the two horses which Karl and Johann had brought to the miller. When she saw them she burst out laughing.

'Do you call those horses?' she demanded. 'They look more like two broken-down donkeys.'

She called her servant to bring forward the magnificent horse he was leading and the miller had to agree that it was the finest horse he had ever seen or heard of.

'Yes,' said the Princess. 'And that horse is for Hans.'

The miller bowed respectfully and said that Hans should have the mill, but the Princess merely laughed again.

'Keep your mill,' she said. 'Hans will have something better.'

She took Hans back to the little summer-house he had built for her and it had turned into a great castle full of gold and silver and bronze. The Princess and Hans were married and Hans sent for the miller's cats, and he did not forget the little cat in the inn, either. And there, by the meadow, they lived happily for the rest of their lives.

Mice do not like this story, but all cats do, and if you ever see two or three cats sitting together in the sunshine or before the fire, purring and blinking their eyes, then you can be sure that they are telling the story of the poor miller's-lad and the Cat Princess. And now you know this story, don't ever believe that just because a lad does not seem clever he will never become important.

Doctor Knowall

Once there was a man called Crab. He had a farm but it was only a small one and the land was so poor that he could barely scratch a living from it.

One rainy day Crab chopped some wood, loaded it on to a cart, harnessed two oxen, and drove into the nearby town. All day he plodded through the muddy streets shouting, 'Firewood, firewood for sale. Good firewood, going cheap.'

Towards evening a doctor called to Crab and said that he would buy the firewood for two pounds.

Two pounds isn't much, thought Crab, but it's the only offer I've had all day so I might as well take it. Something is better than nothing.

Crab unloaded the wood in the doctor's backyard then went to the door to be paid. The doctor was going to have his dinner and when Crab looked through the window he saw roast beef and mashed potatoes and peas, a big jam tart, and a bottle of wine, all spread out on a snowy table-cloth.

'My word,' Crab said. 'That's not bad. That's not bad at all. All I will get for my dinner is a bowl of boiled turnips.'

The doctor came to the window and Crab saw how well-dressed he was. Goodness, Crab thought. There is the doctor dressed in a fine coat and white linen and soft leather shoes, while I'm standing here wet through and dressed in rags. I wouldn't mind being a doctor myself if this is how they live.

The doctor gave Crab two pounds and Crab scratched his nose. 'Tell me,' he said, 'could I be a doctor?'

The doctor looked at Crab standing in the rain in his rags. Another crackpot, he thought. The world is full of them. But to get rid of Crab he said, 'Oh yes, you can become a doctor, it's quite easy. First of all you must buy an ABC book with pictures in it. There is one you can get in this town with a cock on the front. Buy that. Then you must sell your cart and oxen and buy yourself some decent clothes, and make sure you get a long white coat and a stethoscope. Then have a sign painted saying, ''I am Doctor Knowall'', and stick it up over your front door.'

He slammed the window in Crab's face and sat down to his dinner although he could hardly eat for laughing.

However, Crab did what the doctor had told him and for a little while he actually was a doctor, because poor people who could not afford a real doctor went to him. Crab would put on his long, white coat and listen to their chests through his stethoscope, although he had no idea what he was listening for, and then he would look at his ABC book, although he had no idea what the words said, and then he gave the patients coloured water for medicine and, because they knew no better, they drank it and thanked Crab for being good to them, which he was, really, because he did not charge the poor people too much money.

121

Now at the other end of the country there was a Duke who was very rich. One day the Duke found out that a lot of his money had been stolen. The police came but they could not find out who the thief was. Then the Duke got a private detective but he could not find the thief, either. The Duke was terribly angry, but one day his gamekeeper told him about Doctor Knowall.

'Doctor Knowall?' roared the Duke. 'Who's he when he's at home?'

'Ah,' said the gamekeeper. 'He's Doctor Knowall, see. He knows everything.'

'Does he?' the Duke said. 'Well, bring him here and he can tell me who the thief is.'

The gamekeeper took a carriage and went to Doctor Knowall's and gave him the Duke's message.

'All right,' said Knowall, 'I'll come, but only if my wife, Greta, can come too.'

The gamekeeper said that would be all right, so Knowall and his wife got into the carriage and drove to the Duke's mansion. When they got there it was dinner time and the Duke, Knowall, and Greta sat down at the table together.

The Duke rang a bell and a servant came in with the soup. Knowall nudged his wife in the ribs.

'This is the first,' he said, meaning that the soup was the first course. But the servant thought that Knowall was talking about him and that Knowall meant that he was the first thief—which he was!

The servant ran into the kitchen where the other servants were. 'Oh,' he cried. 'It is true. The Doctor knows everything. He took one look at me and said that I was the first thief!'

The second servant was so frightened that he did

not want to go into the dining-room, but the Duke rang the bell again and so he had to go in with a plateful of fish.

As he entered, Knowall nudged Greta again. 'That is the second,' he said, meaning that the fish was the second course. But the servant thought that Knowall was saying that he was the second thief—which he was! He was so terrified that he scampered into the kitchen where he almost fainted and had to drink a bottle of the Duke's best wine!

The third servant took in the meat and again Knowall nudged his wife. 'That is the third,' he said, and the servant thought that Knowall was saying that he was the third thief, which he was!

Then it was the turn of the fourth servant. With his knees knocking he took in a dish, but this dish had a cover over it.

The servant put the dish before the Duke. The Duke looked at the dish and then at Knowall. 'I think that it is about time this Doctor told me something,' he said to himself. 'All he has done so far is sit there eating my food, digging his wife in the ribs, and counting. I will give him a test.'

The Duke leaned forward and tapped the dish with his fork. 'Now, Doctor,' he said. 'You are supposed to know everything. Tell me what is under this cover?'

Knowall had no more idea what was under the cover than the man in the moon. He thought that he was going to be found out and probably given a good whipping for being a fraud. He wiped his forehead with his napkin and rolled his eyes. 'Alas, poor Crab,' he said.

The Duke took off the cover and underneath it on the dish was a roast crab! 'Wonderful!' he cried. 'Wonderful!

This man knows everything. He knows who the thieves are who stole my money.'

The servant who had brought in the roast crab moaned when he heard that. He made a signal to Knowall to follow him into the kitchen. When Knowall went there the servants burst out crying and confessed that they had stolen the money.

'We will tell you where it is hidden,' they said. 'It is behind the stove in the dining-room. But please do not tell the Duke we stole it or we will be hanged.'

'Very well,' said Knowall. 'I don't want to see you hanged. But you must never steal again.'

He went back into the dining-room and sat down. 'Now, Duke,' he said, 'I will tell you where your money is hidden.'

To impress the Duke he picked up his ABC book. I will look in here, he thought, and the Duke will think that I have found the answer in the book. Yes, I will find the cock and pretend that it has told me.

He turned the pages but he could not find the page with the cock on. At last he shouted, 'I know where you are, you had better come out!'

At that the fifth servant, who had been hiding behind the stove, jumped up. 'It is true,' he called. 'The Doctor does know everything!'

Then Knowall showed the Duke where the money was, although he did not say who the thieves were. The Duke was so pleased that he gave Knowall a large reward and the servants gave the Doctor some money, as well.

So Doctor Knowall and his wife went home with plenty of money and they lived well and happily for the rest of their lives.

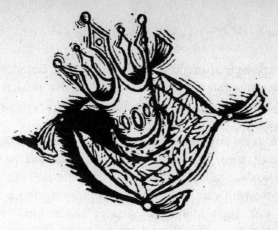

Sleeping Beauty

There was once a king and a queen who had everything that their hearts could desire except a child of their own. Each year they hoped for one but each year slipped away and they remained childless.

Then, one summer's day, the Queen went bathing in a lake. As she was bathing a frog popped its head out of the water, looked at her through its goggle eyes, and croaked, 'Queen, be happy. Before the year is out you will have a child of your own.'

The frog's words came true and by Christmas the Queen had a baby daughter who was so beautiful that all the years of waiting seemed worthwhile. The King was so happy that he gave a great feast. All his family came and all his friends, and all the important people in his Kingdom. He invited the Wise Women of the land, as well.

These Wise Women had magical powers. They knew all the secrets of Heaven and Earth and they had great powers over the birds and the beasts, and over humans, too. The King and the Queen were anxious that the Wise Women should come to their feast so that they would be friendly to their daughter.

There were thirteen wise women in the Kingdom. The trouble was that the King had only twelve golden plates for them to eat from, and so one Wise Woman had to be left out.

The feast was the most magnificent that the Kingdom had ever seen. There was a banquet and fireworks, an opera and a ballet, and a ball. After the ball the guests came forward and hung their presents on the Christmas tree and then they all stepped back and waited, respectfully, as the Wise Women stood in turn by the Princess's cradle and, one by one, gave the child a magical gift. One gave wisdom, another gave virtue, a third gave charity, and so on until the baby had everything that anyone in this world could desire.

Eleven of the twelve Wise Women had given their gifts and the twelfth Wise Woman was about to give hers when, outside, there was a shriek, like an owl seizing a mouse. The window crashed open and a wind, so cold that it might have blown from the North Pole, howled into the room. Everyone turned around and there, standing in the window, her eyes glinting as green as emeralds in her white face, stood the thirteenth Wise Woman!

She raised her hands above her head and it seemed as if her blood-red nails were claws. 'Hear me,' she cried, and her voice was like a spoon scraping a pan. 'Hear me. You would not invite me to the party but I have come just the same. Yes, and I have brought a present, too. On her fifteenth birthday the Princess will prick her finger on a spindle of a spinning-wheel and she will fall down dead!'

Then, in a gust of wind, she vanished.

The King and Queen and all the guests were horrified. The King went white and the Queen held her hand to her breast as if a poisoned dagger had been plunged there.

But then the twelfth Wise Woman stepped forward. 'Do not despair,' she said. 'I have not yet given my gift. Although I cannot undo the curse that woman has placed on the child, there is one thing I can do. The Princess will certainly prick her finger on a spindle when she is fifteen but she will not die. No, she will not die; she will sleep, for a hundred years.'

That very night the King ordered that every spindle in the land should be burned, and he ordered that if any man, woman, or child hid a spindle they were to be put to death. But there was no need for that threat. The whole Kingdom felt sorrow for the King and Queen and their baby daughter, and so they burned their spindles so that the child should not be harmed.

And so the child grew, and as she grew the gifts of the Wise Women grew with her, so that she was wise and beautiful and virtuous and kind. Then came her fifteenth birthday.

The Princess woke early, and, while she waited for breakfast, she wandered around the palace. She thought that she knew every nook and cranny, but, in the attic, behind an old wardrobe, she found a tiny door which she had never seen before.

She opened this door, squeezed through it, and found herself in a long corridor, inches thick with dust, and festooned with cobwebs. The Princess wandered down the corridor watched by spiders and mice, and then she came to a strange, arched doorway. She turned the latch and pressed, the door creaked open and the Princess crept inside. She was in a room without windows and where there was no lamp; yet it was light, and in the middle of the room the Princess saw an old woman spinning flax into linen thread.

'Good morning, Mother,' said the Princess.

The woman turned her head around and her face looked older than time itself. It was wrinkled and withered, like an ancient cliff, and her eyes were blind.

'What are you doing, Mother?' the Princess asked.

The old woman smiled. 'I am waiting for you, my child. I am spinning and waiting for you.'

'And what are you spinning?' asked the Princess.

'Thread, my dear,' said the old one.

The Princess took a step forward. 'And what is the thread for?'

The old woman smiled, but there was a dark hole behind her lips. 'It is for a sheet, my dear.'

'What sort of a sheet?'

The old one cackled and clapped her bony hands together. 'It is a winding-sheet!'

The Princess took another step forward and looked at the spindle which leaped and jerked at the end of the thread. 'And what is that which dances so merrily?' she asked, and she touched the spindle and pricked her finger and the curse became true, and she fell down in a deep sleep.

As the Princess fell, the King and the Queen fell asleep, too, and all the courtiers with them. The horses in the stables fell asleep, and the dappled dogs in the yard. The doves in the dovecote slept, the hens in the coop, and the cows in the byre. The cook, who was pulling the hair of an idle servant boy, fell asleep, and the lad with her. The flies on the midden closed their eyes, and the bees in the flowers. Even the fire ceased to flicker, although the flames were as red as ever. The wind died away, not a leaf on the trees stirred, and all the clocks stopped.

The months passed away, and the years, and around the palace, beyond the reach of the spell, a hedge of wild roses began to grow. Each year it grew higher and higher until it grew above the roof of the palace and hid it so that nothing could be seen, not even the King's standard on the topmost tower.

But although the palace and all within it were lost in a timeless dream, and although it, and all within it, were hidden by a bank of green, the story of the sleeping Princess spread across the world. Many a fine lad heard of the Princess, who was called the Sleeping Beauty, and many a fine lad tried to break through the briar hedge to find her.

All failed. The briars had grown together and the tendrils curled and writhed about each other, and as the bold lads struggled through the hedge the tendrils curled about them, too; and the briar thorns, as sharp and curved and long as eagles' beaks, hooked into them and held them fast so that they died there and their skeletons could be seen gleaming in the winter's sun.

One day, after many a long year had passed, a Prince came into the country. In a tavern he heard an old, old man tell of the great briar hedge, and that behind it there was said to be a palace, and that in the palace there was a beauty who had been sleeping for many years.

'Why,' said the Prince. 'A hedge is only a hedge. I will break through it and waken the Princess.'

The old man shook his head. 'No, no,' he cried. 'My grandfather told me that many a lad has tried but all of them were caught in the hedge and died there. Do not join them. Remember your father and mother. Do you want them to mourn for you?'

But the lad had the blood of youth in his heart and

although he thanked the old man for his kind warning, he went to the hedge the next day.

His sword in his hand, the Prince began to hack through the briars. All day he chopped and slashed at the thorns, and the thorns chopped and slashed at him so that his face and hands were bloody and torn. Deep in the hedge the skulls of the other bold lads grinned mockingly at him but he fought on and, towards evening, the tendrils became softer and the thorns smaller, until, as the sun sank to the west, he burst from the hedge and found himself in the palace.

He wiped the blood from his face and looked around. There he saw the dappled hounds, all fast asleep, and the horses and the cows with them. In the dovecote the doves were perched with their heads underneath their wings and the flies were asleep on the midden. The cook still held the servant lad by the hair and by the silent fire a kitchen-maid was sitting, a black hen in her hands.

The Prince went into the Great Hall of the palace. The courtiers were standing there, as still as statues, and one of them was bowing before the King and Queen who were fast asleep on their thrones. The Prince tiptoed through the palace until he came to the attics. He found the passage way, where the mice and spiders were sleeping, and he found the strange door, opened it, and went into the room which had light without windows or a lamp. And there, lying on the floor, covered with a winding-sheet, was the Sleeping Beauty.

The Prince pulled the winding-sheet away and looked at the Princess's face.

'Ah,' he whispered, 'Princess, if only you could waken then I would marry you,' and he leaned forward and kissed her on the cheek.

And as the Prince kissed the Princess he heard a clock chime. Why, he thought, that is strange. Everything should be under the spell.

But as the clock chimed the Princess's eyelids fluttered and her lips opened. The clock chimed again until it had struck nine times, and on the stroke of nine the hundred years had come to an end and the spell was broken.

The Princess woke up and all the court with her. The spiders began to spin their webs, the mice ran to their holes, the dogs barked and wagged their tails, the horses neighed, the doves flew into the air, the flies buzzed, the cook gave the lazy servant lad a box on the ears, the maid finished plucking the black hen, the flames of the fire crackled away merrily, and the great hedge burst into roses.

The Prince took the Princess down from the attics into the Great Hall. The King and the Queen and all the court were yawning and stretching their arms but as the Princess walked in they all cried, 'Happy birthday,' and a happy birthday it was.

That is the story of the Sleeping Beauty. When she was twenty-one she married the Prince and, later, became Queen and had children of her own. But of one thing you can be certain. She always made sure that she had enough plates for all her guests!

The Bremen Town Musicians

In the days before tigers had stripes, a man in Germany had a donkey. The donkey had worked for the man for many years, but, as the years passed away, he became old and feeble and his master began to look at him with a far-away look in his eyes.

The donkey thought he knew what that look meant, and when, one day, he saw his master talking to the butcher, he was sure.

'They aren't going to turn me into cats'-meat,' he snickered, and that night he kicked down the stable door and trotted off into the night. He spent the night in a field wondering what to do and, as the moon set, he had an idea. I know, he thought, I will go to the famous city of Bremen and become a town musician. Then he ate some thistles and went to sleep.

The next morning he set off along the highway. Before he had gone very far he came across a big dog lying on the road, panting as if it had run a hundred miles non-stop.

The donkey stood still. 'Now then, old Barker,' he said, 'what's the matter with you?'

The dog raised its weary head. 'Ah,' it gasped, 'I have served my master faithfully for eleven years, but now that I am grown old, and my legs are rheumaticky, and I cannot chase the deer any more, he has been saying that he would have me killed, and so I have run away. But what I will do now I cannot say. How will I live?'

The donkey shook his head. 'Terrible, isn't it? It's just the same with me. But listen, I'm going to Bremen to be a town musician. Why not come along? I'll beat the drum and you can play the lute.'

'That's a good idea,' said the dog, and it trotted along behind the donkey.

After a while they came to a wood where they met a cat which had a face as long as a week of wet Sundays.

'Look here,' said the donkey, 'what's wrong, Whiskers? Cheer up now.'

'Mkreeow,' miaowed the cat. 'It's all right talking, but it isn't easy to be cheerful when you are down and out. I used to be a fine young cat but now my teeth are worn down and my claws are blunt. Nowadays I like to sit by the fire instead of galloping about catching mice, so my Mistress said that she was going to drown me in the well. I've cleared off, but what is going to happen to me now? There isn't much future in this world for an old cat, I can tell you.'

'I know the story,' the donkey said. 'Old Barker, here, and I are in the same state. But why not come along with us to Bremen? We are going to be town musicians and you can be one, too. After all, if anyone is good at night music it has to be you, hasn't it?'

The cat cheered up when she heard the donkey. 'Thanks very much,' she purred. 'I'll be glad to join you.' And she washed her face and followed the donkey and the dog.

The three runaways jogged on until they came to a farmyard where a cock was perched upon a gate, crowing with all its might and main.

'Goodness,' said the donkey. 'That crowing goes through me like a needle. What's the matter, old Redcomb?'

'What's the use,' said the cock. 'What's the use of being pious? All week I have been crowing for good weather for Lady Day, when Our Lady washes the Christ child's shirts and needs the sun to dry them, and what happens? The farmer's wife has some friends coming on Sunday and she has told the cook to wring my neck and boil me up into soup. That's why I am crowing now, it is my last chance.'

'That's gratitude for you,' said the donkey. 'That's what humans are like. But why wait to have your neck wrung? Come along with us, we are all in the same boat but we are going to Bremen to be town musicians. You have a big voice and when we all get together and practise for a bit we will have a fine band.'

'Thank you,' said the cock. 'Thank you very much. It's certainly better than ending up in the soup-pot,' and he crowed once more, then hopped down from the gate, and the four beasts went down the Bremen road in search of a comfortable old age.

However, time was getting on, and the four friends could not get to Bremen that day. When night fell they came to a forest and decided to sleep there. The donkey and the dog settled down under a tree and the cock and the cat climbed up into the branches. The cock liked to be as high up as he could get because it felt safer, and he hopped and fluttered to the very top of the tree and perched there. Then the donkey brayed 'goodnight', the dog woofed, the cat miaowed, and the cock gave a last crow. But before the cock tucked his head under his wing he had a last look around and in the distance he saw a spark of light.

'Comrades,' he called. 'I think that there is a house nearby.'

The donkey swivelled its long ears. 'That is good news,' he said. 'Let's go and see if we can get shelter. The night dew is beginning to make my old bones ache.'

The animals agreed. The dog thought that he might be given a juicy bone, the cat hoped she might get a bowl of milk, the cock would not have said no to a handful of wheat, and the donkey fancied a few carrots, so off they went.

They plunged through the forest and soon they came upon a house with a bright light streaming from the window. The animals crept up to the house and the donkey stretched up its neck and peeped through the window.

'What do you see, Neddy?' asked the dog.

'What do I see?' The donkey drew back its lips from its long, yellow teeth. 'I see a table crammed with good food and drink.'

He rolled his eyes at his friends. The dog wagged his tail, the cat arched its back, and the cock clicked its beak.

'Yes,' whispered the donkey. 'There is a table covered with good things—only there are six robbers sitting around it and eating them.'

'Six robbers?' the cat mewed, and it darted away into the trees followed by the dog, the cock, and the donkey.

'Robbers,' said the cock. 'My word, I'm all of a tremble.'

'Me too,' the dog growled. 'But I must say, that food would just suit me.'

'And me,' said the donkey. 'But how are we to get rid of the robbers?'

In the light of the moon the animals put their heads together and tried to think of a way to get at the food. In the end the clever cat had an idea.

'I know,' she said to the donkey. 'Neddy, go to the window and put your front legs on the window-sill. The dog will stand on your back. I will stand on the dog and the cock can stand on me. Then, when the cock crows we will—' And she whispered the rest of her plan. When she had finished the animals nodded their heads in agreement, tiptoed back to the house, and the dog and the cat and the cock climbed on to the donkey's back.

'Now then,' cried the cock. 'Let them hear the Bremen Town Musicians!' He crowed as if the town was on fire, the donkey hee-hawed like a circular saw, the dog howled like a soul in torment, and the cat wailed like a banshee. Then they all jumped through the window, screeching and howling as if they were the hounds of Hell let loose.

The robbers thought that a demon was after them. They jumped up and dashed away into the forest. The animals burst out laughing, went into the house, and tucked into the food on the table. When they had finished they thanked God for his mercies, put out the light, and settled down to sleep, each finding the bed which suited its nature. The donkey in the yard by a warm midden, the dog behind the door, the cat in the hearth, and the cock on the rafters. Then, tired as they were, they closed their eyes and slept.

An hour passed, and another. The stars shone down and far away a church clock struck midnight. In the forest the robber chief shook his head.

'Eeeh, lads,' he said. 'This won't do. This won't do at

all. My word, if the other robbers in the forest get to hear of this they will never stop laughing. By gum, they will say that we are nowt but a pack of schoolgirls, not a band of desperate robbers. We must do something.'

The other robbers were silent. They scratched their hair and rubbed their noses and stared at the moon, but none of them spoke. Finally the robber chief struck his fist on his knee.

'I know,' he said. He turned to a little robber. 'Go and find out what is happening in the house,' he said. 'Don't worry, we'll be right behind you.'

'Thanks for nothing,' said the little robber, but because he was more afraid of the robber chief whom he knew, than the strange noises which he didn't, he crept across the moonlit glade to the house, opened the door, and slid inside. He was very quiet, but the cat, which could hear mice a hundred yards away, heard him and opened its eyes. Her eyes glowed so brightly that the robber thought that they were burning coals. He crept across the kitchen and poked a twig into the cat's eyes so that he would have a light. But the cat did not find that funny. With a hiss it leaped at the robber's face and raked four deep scratches down his cheek.

The robber screamed and ran for the back door, but the dog, which was lying there, bit his ankle. The robber stumbled through the door into the yard and the donkey lashed out with its back legs and kicked him, nearly dashing his brains out. To cap it all, the cock woke up, cried, 'Cock-a-doodle doo!' jumped down on to the robber's head and pecked him ten times in the ear.

The robber scrambled back to his mates. 'Clear out,' he shouted. 'Clear out as quick as you can. There is a terrible old witch in the house who spat at me and scratched me with her long fingernails. Behind the door there is a dwarf who stabbed me in the ankle with a knife. In the yard there is a huge, black monster who beat me with a club, and in the rafters there is a judge who shrieked, ''Bring the rogue here and I will hang him!'' '

The robbers screamed with fear and ran away as fast as their legs could carry them, but the four animals were so pleased with their new house that they stayed there and lived together for many a long year, each looking after the other out of the goodness of their hearts. Certainly they never went to Bremen to become town musicians, and now that you have heard this tale you might think that it was lucky for them that they didn't. Yes, and lucky for Bremen, too!

And the mouth of the man who told me this tale is still warm. Believe me.

The Six Swans

O nce, in a faraway land, a king went hunting in a forest and lost his way. As evening drew near he came to a glade and met an old woman and asked her to show him a path back to his palace.

The old woman said that she knew the way but she would show it to the King only on one condition. The King asked what that was and the old woman said that the King would have to marry her daughter. If he would not marry her daughter, then he would have to stay in the forest for ever.

The King looked at the vast and tangled wilderness and knew that he could never find his way on his own and so, in despair, he agreed.

'Very well,' said the old woman. 'You will not be sorry. My daughter is young and beautiful.'

She crept away into the forest and came back with her daughter. It was true what the old woman had said, the daughter was young and beautiful, but when the King looked at her he felt a secret horror. There was something about the girl, a strange light which flickered in her dark eyes, and a strange smile which played across her red lips, which frightened him.

But still, the King had to marry her or die in the forest and so he said he would marry her as soon as he got back to his palace. Then the old woman showed him the way and the King was soon home, and then he married the girl and she became his Queen.

Now the King had been married before and he had six sons and a daughter. But he did not show the children to the new Queen. The strange light in her eyes and the strange smile on her lips made him afraid that if the Queen saw the children she would harm them. So he took the children to a castle in the forest and hid them there. And the way to the castle was so secret that even the King could not have found it but for one thing.

Once the King had been kind to a woman who was a witch, although she was a good witch. The witch had given the King a ball of wool. But it was not an ordinary ball of wool. When it was thrown down it rolled away and showed the way to the castle. Without the wool no one could find the path to the castle and so the King knew that his children were safe.

But the King loved his children so much that he could not bear to be away from them for long and every other day he took the ball of wool, threw it down, and followed it to the castle.

Now the King was away so often that the Queen became curious. She wondered why he was in the forest so much and what he did there, because she did not believe that he was hunting. Whenever the King rode out the Queen stood at a window in a high tower and marked the way he went, but whenever she tried to follow him she got lost and had to ride home again.

The Queen could not rest. Night and day she thought of where the King went, and when she thought of it the strange light flickered in the darkness of her eyes and the strange, twisted smile crossed her lips.

Now one of the King's trusted servants was a villain and the Queen knew this. As they say, like recognizes like, and the Queen bribed the villain to tell her what the King's secret was. The villain took the money and said: 'It's like this. The King has hidden his children in the forest and he goes to see them every other day.'

'Children?' said the Queen. 'I did not know the King had children,' and suddenly her beautiful face looked ancient and withered and evil.

'Oh yes,' said the servant. He took a glass of wine, drank, and wiped his mouth with the back of his hand. 'If you gave me some more gold I could tell a secret about them.'

The Queen gave the man a bag of gold and he told her of the magic ball of wool.

'Get the ball of wool for me,' said the Queen. 'Get it and you can have anything you wish. Anything at all. Anything.'

So the villain stole the ball of wool from the King's study and gave it to the Queen. That night the Queen made seven little shirts, and when she had made them she breathed a magic spell on to them, for it was true what the King had seen the first day he met her: although the Queen was beautiful, she had a dark and twisted heart.

The next morning the King left his castle to go hunting. When he had gone, the Queen went into the forest and threw down the ball of wool and it unwound and led her to the secret castle.

As the Queen rode towards the castle the six boys were playing in the courtyard but the girl was reading in her room. When the boys saw a rider coming towards them they thought the King had come to visit them and they ran forward to greet their father. When they saw the Queen they tried to run away, but it was too late. The Queen threw a magic shirt over each of them and they turned into swans and flew away.

The Queen laughed with delight for now she had no stepchildren and the King would have no one else to love but herself. She followed the woollen ball home to the palace and put it back in the King's room. But she did not know about the little girl!

The next day the King went to the castle. His daughter told him what had happened but he could not bring himself to believe it; not until she showed him a handful of swans' feathers which had drifted from the sky when her brothers had flown away.

Then the King believed her and knew that he had lost his sons, but still he could not believe that it was the Queen who had done such a wicked thing. It must have been some other woman, he thought, and he decided to take his daughter back to the palace with him because he was afraid that the witch might come again and turn her into a swan, too.

But the little Princess burst out crying and asked him to let her stay in the castle in case her brothers came back. She cried so much that in the end the King allowed her to stay for just one more night. He rode away and said that he would return the next day, but he warned her not to leave the castle for anything at all.

All morning the Princess waited in the castle but no swans flew in from the sky, and all afternoon she waited, too. Then she could not bear to wait any longer.

If my dear brothers cannot return to me, then I will go

and find them, she thought and, although the night was coming and the forest was full of wolves and bears, she put on her coat and set off into the wilderness, for that is how much she loved her brothers.

All night the Princess wandered through the forest, calling to her brothers, and all the next day she wandered, too, but there was no answer to her calls, only the howling of wolves and the growling of bears. Finally, at the end of the second day, when she could walk no further, she came upon a tiny house. She went into the house and inside she found six small cots. Although the Princess was very tired she did not dare to lie on the cots and so she lay beneath them and closed her eyes, wondering what the night would bring.

The sun dipped to the horizon but just before it set the Princess heard a strange calling and crying in the sky, and a beating of wings, and from the scarlet sunset came six swans! Yes, six snowy swans flew in through the window, and when they had landed they blew at each other and their feathers floated to the ground and their swans' skins fell from them; and the six swans were the Princess's brothers.

The Princess crept from under the bed and when her brothers saw her they wept—and not for sorrow, you may be sure. But they said that the girl could not stay in the hut.

'This is a robbers' den,' they said, 'and if the robbers find you when they get back they will kill you.'

'Ah,' said the Princess, 'but you will defend me.'

'No,' said the brothers. 'We are only human for fifteen minutes each day. Then we turn back into swans.'

'Oh,' tears came into the Princess's eyes. 'Is there nothing I can do to help you?'

'Yes,' said the brothers, 'yes there is. But it is so hard for you to do that we do not like to ask you.'

'Never mind that,' said the Princess. 'I will do it if it is the hardest thing in the world.'

'Very well,' the brothers answered. 'Then this is what you must do. There is a tiny flower which grows in the woods. It is called the starflower. You must gather the starflowers and sew six shirts for us. That will be hard to do because the flowers are so tiny. In fact it will take you six years but, and this is the hard part, if during those six long years you speak once—even if you only say one word—then we will remain swans until we die. And even if you laugh during those six years then we will stay swans for ever and for ever and for ever.'

'I will do it,' the Princess said, but even as she spoke the brothers turned into swans and spread their wings and flew away to the north, calling with sad, haunting calls.

The little Princess ran from the robbers' hut and went into the forest. All night long she gathered starflowers and the next morning she climbed up a tree and began to make the first shirt. All day long she worked in silence, and all the night long she gathered starflowers, and all the next day she sat in the tree and worked making a shirt, and never a sound crossed her lips. And so, from month to month she lived in the forest.

After a time it happened that the King of the country was hunting in the forest and his huntsmen passed the tree where the girl sat sewing. As you might guess, they were surprised to see her.

'Who are you?' they called. 'What are you doing there?'

The Princess would not utter one word but she thought, I will get rid of them, and she threw down a golden necklace. Still the huntsmen would not go. Then the Princess threw down her cloak, and her robe, and her gown, until all she had on was her petticoat.

But the huntsmen shook their heads. 'You are in our King's forest,' they said. 'You must go before him and answer for yourself.' They climbed the tree and brought the Princess down and took her to the King.

The King was amazed to see such a beautiful girl in the middle of his forest but, although he asked who she was and why she was there, she was as silent as a stone.

The King was moved by the girl's beauty. He wrapped her in his cloak, and placed her on his own horse, and took her to his palace where, even though she would not speak one word, he married her.

The King's mother was jealous of the beautiful girl and spoke evil things about her. 'Who is this girl?' she asked. 'No one knows where she is from or who she is. Why does she spend all her time gathering starflowers unless she is a witch? And why will she not speak unless she has something wicked to hide? She is not worthy to be a Queen.'

However, the King would not listen to his mother and he was happy with his strange wife. Then there came a time when the Queen had a child, a baby boy, and the King rejoiced in his son. But the King's mother was so evil, and hated the Queen so much, that, one night, she stole the child from its cradle and gave it to a woodcutter. Then she killed a chicken and spread its blood on the Queen's mouth and she told the King that his wife was a witch who had eaten her own baby.

But the King loved his wife so much that he would not believe this. 'No, no,' he cried. 'Someone else has stolen the child and tried to blame it on my Queen.'

145

As for the Queen, she did not say one word but carried on making the six shirts from starflowers.

By and by the Queen had another child, a beautiful daughter. Once again the King's mother stole the child and gave it to the woodcutter and killed a chicken and smeared the Queen's mouth with its blood. But once again the King would not believe her, and as for the Queen, she spoke not one word but continued making star shirts.

And then, for the third time, the Queen had a child, and for the third time the King's mother stole the child and smeared blood on the Queen's mouth and accused her of eating her own child. The King tried to defend his Queen. He sent for her and asked her to deny the charge.

'Just say one word,' he pleaded. 'Just say, no. That will be enough.'

But the Queen would not utter a word and knelt before him sewing her star shirts for her brothers. The King groaned and wrung his hands but he could do nothing more and so the Queen was found guilty and sentenced to death by burning at the stake.

The Queen was taken away and locked in a dungeon full of snakes and rats until the day came when she was to be taken to the stake, and that day was the last day of the six years she had been given to make the star shirts. The Queen had worked so hard that she had finished five of the shirts and the sixth shirt was almost completed. Only the left sleeve needed sewing and she was doing that when the door of the dungeon opened, and the executioner stood there in his mask and crooked his finger for her to follow him and go to the stake to be burned.

The Queen draped the shirts over her arm, and even as she walked to the stake she was sewing the sixth shirt. The King begged her to speak and say that she was innocent but still the Queen would not say one word, although when she looked at the King the tears spilled from her eyes and ran down her cheeks. Even the executioner was sorry for her as he tied her to the stake and piled up the wood around her. But still, she was to be burned, and so he struck flint against steel and lit a brand. Then, just as he was about to light the fire, there was a trumpeting in the sky and down swooped the six swans!

The Queen struggled an arm free and threw the star shirts over the swans and they were turned back into her brothers, all except the youngest, for he caught the unfinished shirt and so, all his life, instead of a left arm he had a silver swan's wing.

The brothers freed the Queen and then she was able to speak. She told the King what had happened to her and how the King's mother had stolen the children. The King sent for the woodcutter who brought the three children from the forest, and they were strong and well. And as for the King's mother, she was taken to the stake instead of the Queen and burned for her wickedness. And so, after six long, silent years, the King and the Queen, and the six brothers, and the Queen's three children were happy and they lived out their lives together in peace and contentment.

The Mouse, the Bird,
and the Sausage

I n the days before the birds chose their King, a sparrow, a mouse, and a sausage became friends and decided to set up house together.

Each of the three did a fair share of the work. Every morning the sparrow flew into the woods and brought back twigs for the fire, the mouse went to the stream for water, and the sausage did the cooking. Together the three creatures lived happily and well.

One day the sparrow met a chaffinch and boasted of how well off and happy it was. The chaffinch was jealous. It clicked its beak and looked at the sparrow out of the corner of its little yellow eye.

'I don't know what you are so pleased about,' it said. 'It seems to me that you have got the worst job. The mouse has only to go to the stream, and that isn't very far, and it can bring back enough water to last the day so then it goes into its hole and sleeps. And take that sausage: all it does is put the vegetables in the pot, jump in with them, and make sure that they are well stirred by rolling around in the hot water. Then it can go to sleep in the colander. But you . . . well, I'm not trying to make trouble . . . but you have to go miles for the twigs, and they're heavy to carry. I don't like to mention it but your beak is getting all droopy. I'll bet the mouse and sausage are laughing at you behind your back. I know all the other birds are.'

And having done its mischief the chaffinch flew away.

All night the sparrow brooded over what the chaffinch had said and the next morning it told the sausage and the mouse that it was not going to gather firewood any more.

'We'll have to change,' it cheeped. 'Let one of you two get the wood.'

The mouse and the sausage were sorry to hear this and begged the sparrow to change its mind, but it would not. In fact the more they begged the sparrow the more it thought that the chaffinch was right and that the other two had the easiest jobs.

In the end the sausage and the mouse agreed to change jobs. To make sure that everything was fair they agreed that they would draw lots. They took scraps of paper and wrote down their names and they also wrote down the names of the jobs. Then they put the papers in the sausage's hat and drew them out with their eyes closed. When they looked at the papers they found that the sausage was to get the twigs, the mouse became cook, and the sparrow was to bring the water.

The next morning the little sausage rolled off to the woods to get firewood, the sparrow flew to the stream, and the mouse peeled the vegetables for the dinner. But the day slipped away and the sausage did not return with the firewood. Finally, in the afternoon, the sparrow flew off to find the sausage.

The sparrow fluttered along the lane and by a stile it met a big dog.

'Excuse me, dog,' chirped the sparrow. 'Have you seen a sausage around here?'

The dog yawned. 'Oh yes,' it said.

'Do you know where it is now, please?' asked the sparrow.

'Yes,' said the dog and patted its stomach. 'It's in here.'

The sparrow almost fainted. 'Do you mean . . . do you mean you have eaten it?'

The dog yawned again. 'That's right.'

'But . . . but . . .' the sparrow trembled. 'But that's murder!'

'No, no.' The dog shook its big head. 'The sausage was carrying forged pound notes and round here you can be killed for that, so I did it.' He licked his lips and looked at the sparrow. 'Do you have any forged pound notes on you—' But the sparrow had already flown away.

When the sparrow got home it told the mouse what had happened to the poor sausage and they both sat around the table, crying. But although they had lost their friend life had to go on and they agreed to stay together and do the best they could. So, the next day, the sparrow went for the twigs and the water, and the mouse put the vegetables in the pan. When the water was boiling the mouse remembered that the sausage used to jump in the pan and roll around with the vegetables to make sure that they were done properly. Before the sparrow could stop her, she had jumped in the pan and inside a second she had lost her little life.

The sparrow tried to get the mouse out of the pot but she knocked the pot on to the fire. The burning wood was scattered over the floor and set fire to the house. The sparrow dashed to the well for water but she was so flustered that she fell down the well with the bucket and was drowned.

And that was the end of the mouse, the sparrow, and the sausage. Remember it if ever anyone tells you bad tales about your friends.

Little Red Riding-Hood

Not far from Tom Thumb's house there lived a man, his wife, and their daughter. She was such a bright, cheerful child that everyone liked her. For a birthday present her grannie made her a hood of red velvet, such as ladies wear when they go riding. The child liked the hood so much that she wore it everywhere she went. The people in the district would see the little red hood bobbing along and smile, and they called the girl little Red Riding-Hood.

One day Red Riding-Hood's mother said to her, 'My dear, your grannie is not very well. I can't get over today because it is washing day, but in this basket there is some cake and wine. Take them for me and say I'm sorry for not coming but I will call over tomorrow.'

The girl took the basket and put on her hood but at the cottage door her mother held her for a moment. 'Now,' she said, 'don't go hopping and skipping about or you might fall and hurt yourself, and you might break the bottle, too. Stay on the path and remember, don't talk to any strangers.'

'Yes, mother,' said Red Riding-Hood. She set off and, remembering her promise, she walked slowly and kept to the path.

Red Riding-Hood's grannie lived in a wood, about two miles away. As the child entered the shade of the trees she saw a wolf sitting on the path, blocking her way. She gave a little scream but the wolf grinned at her and wagged his tail, as if he was a playful puppy.

'Good morning, my dear,' he said.

The wolf looked so friendly and he spoke so nicely, that Red Riding-Hood forgot her promise to her mother. 'Good morning,' she answered.

'And where are you going, little one?' the wolf asked.

'I am going to my grannie,' Red Riding-Hood said. 'She is poorly.'

'Is she now?' The wolf pricked up his ears. 'And where does your grannie live, little girl?'

'In the wood,' Red Riding-Hood said. 'In a cottage by two nut trees. Surely you know it?'

'Oh yes,' said the wolf. 'By two nut trees, yes. Yes, I know it. That's a nice little old lady living there, right enough. Er . . . does she live alone?'

'All alone,' said Red Riding-Hood.

Two red sparks glowed at the back of the wolf's dark eyes. 'And where are your mother and father?'

'My mother is washing,' said Red Riding-Hood. 'And my father is in the town buying a cow.'

'Is he now?' said the wolf. His nose twitched and he thought, Well, this is a bit of luck. He looked at Red Riding-Hood and his long, red tongue slid over his yellow fangs. 'What a plump young creature,' he said to himself. 'She is as tender as a young chicken. Mmm, I can taste her now, so I can, better than an old bag of bones like her grannie. Still, I will be crafty and get them both. Yes. I wonder which one I should eat first?'

He stood up and stretched himself and smiled at Red Riding-Hood who smiled back. 'I'll tell you what I will do,' he said. 'I will walk through the wood with you and see you safe and sound. There are some bad types lurking about round here but you will be safe with me.'

'Thank you,' said Red Riding-Hood. 'My mother told me to be careful.'

'Very sensible,' the wolf said, but he turned his head aside and his body shook with laughter.

Together, the wolf and Red Riding-Hood walked through the woods. The birds whistled and chirped, 'Red Riding-Hood, Red Riding-Hood, run away home,' but she could not understand their language and so she walked beside the wolf, patting his rough neck.

After a little while the wolf said, 'Missy, why do you walk with your eyes glued to the path. Goodness, you look as if you are going back to school after the holidays. Look around you. See how beautiful the woods are.'

Red Riding-Hood looked up, and when she saw the sunbeams dancing through the trees, and the dew sparkling on the grass, she said, 'I think that I ought to take Grannie some flowers. That would please her.'

'I'm sure that they would,' said the wolf. He pointed to a glade. 'Look, there are some pretty bluebells.'

Red Riding-Hood ran from the path and gathered the flowers. Then the wolf cried out:

'And look, little one, further on, there. Yes, those flowers are even more beautiful.'

Red Riding-Hood ran to those flowers and picked them. Then she saw another bank of blossom and she ran for those, and so she went deeper and deeper into the wood until she was lost to sight. Then the wolf gave a terrible growl and loped off to the grannie's cottage.

When he got there he knocked at the door and a creaky, trembling voice asked who was there.

The wolf gave a simpering smile. 'It is Red Riding-Hood, Grannie,' he said in a high-pitched voice. 'I have brought you cake and wine and some lovely flowers.'

'Lift the latch, my dear one,' called Grannie. 'Lift the latch and walk in.'

'Yes, Grannie,' said the wolf. 'Thank you, Grannie,' and he lifted the latch, walked in, sprang on the bed, and swallowed down Red Riding-Hood's grannie in one huge gulp. Then he rummaged in the wardrobe and found a night-gown and a nightcap. He put them on, jumped into bed, pulled the bedclothes over his nose—and waited.

Deep in the woods Red Riding-Hood had gathered as many flowers as she could carry and was running to the cottage. When she got there she was surprised to see the door open. She peered round the door and saw a pink nightcap sticking up from the bedclothes. 'Grannie,' she whispered, and she tiptoed to the bed.

'Good morning, Grannie,' she said, remembering her manners, but she felt uneasy, although she could not say why. She sat down beside the bed. 'How strange you look, Grannie,' she said. 'What big ears you have, today.'

'All the better to hear you with,' said the wolf.

'And what big eyes you have, Grannie.'

'All the better to see you with.'

'And what big hands you have, Grannie.'

'All the better to hug you with.'

'And what big teeth you have, Grannie.'

'All the better to eat you with!'

And with one bound the wolf was out of the bed and had swallowed Red Riding-Hood!

The wolf smacked his lips and drank the bottle of wine. He felt very full; after all, he had both Grannie and Red Riding-Hood inside him, and he felt tired too so he lay down on the bed and fell asleep.

After a little while he began to snore. Louder and louder he snored until the plates clattered on the dresser and the window panes rattled. The drone of the snores drifted out through the window. The birds heard it and they twittered with laughter, and the deer heard it and they laughed, and a huntsman heard it, too.

The huntsman cocked his head. That's strange, he thought. Those snores are coming from the old lady's cottage. I wonder if she is all right.

He spurred his horse through the trees, went into the cottage, and there he saw the wolf sound asleep on the bed.

'Aha!' cried the huntsman. 'It is you is it, you old sinner? I have wanted to catch you these many years past. Right!'

He lifted his musket and was about to fire when he saw something move in the wolf's stomach. Hello, he thought, I wonder if—yes—I'll bet that is the old lady in there, and she is still alive!

He picked up a pair of sewing scissors and snipped at the wolf's skin. Snip, snip, he went and saw a little red hood. He snipped again and out jumped Red Riding-Hood. The huntsman snipped three more times and out tumbled Grannie, who was so squashed up she could hardly breathe.

The huntsman went into the garden and picked up some heavy stones. He stuffed them into the wolf's belly

156

then stitched up the cut. Just as he had finished sewing the wolf woke up. He howled and jumped through the window and ran away. But when he came to a stream he was so heavy that he fell into the water and was drowned.

The huntsman laughed and took the wolf's skin. Grannie got back into bed and had her cake and a nice cup of tea, and Red Riding-Hood ran home and said to herself:

'As long as I live I will never leave the path, or speak to strangers, and I will do as my mother tells me, like a good little girl.'

Now there may not be any wolves where you live, but think of Red Riding-Hood when you go for a walk.

The Singing Bone

Once, in a faraway land, there was a huge and savage boar which ravaged the entire countryside. The boar was so dreadful that people were afraid to go out in case it caught them and ripped them to pieces with its terrible yellow tusks, and so the fields were left untilled, no crops were grown, there was no food to be had, and all the shops were empty.

After two or three years, things got so bad that people were dying of hunger. Aye, children lay in the gutters and died there, and their fathers and mothers died with them. In his castle on a steep crag, the King of the country looked down on his suffering people and, because he loved them, and because they could not pay their rents, he sent out his heralds who sounded their trumpets in every village and town in the land where, dressed in their green and gold livery, and mounted on fine white horses, they gave this message to the people: 'In the name of the King! Whoever kills the wild boar may marry the King's daughter, the Princess Katerina!'

The trumpets sounded their brazen message across the Kingdom, in the greatest city and in the remotest village and they sounded, too, on the very edge of the forest where the wild boar lived.

Now on the edge of the forest there lived two brothers, Karl and Fritz, and they heard the trumpets and the King's message and both of them longed to kill the wild boar and marry the Princess. The older brother, Karl, was cunning and sly and a cheat, but the younger brother, Fritz, was innocent and trusting and good-hearted. If a poor beggar came to their door, Karl would kick him away and set the dogs on him, but Fritz would always go after the poor beggar and give him a few pence and a bit of bread and cheese and wish him luck; yes, even if Fritz had no money himself and was hungry, he would do that out of the goodness of his innocent heart.

Anyway, when the brothers heard the King's message they both decided to go into the forest, right into the boar's lair, and find it and kill it. But, although Karl wanted to do this so that he could marry the Princess, Fritz wanted to do it to save the poor people of the Kingdom from starvation. That was the sort of pure-hearted lad he was, and that's a fact.

Now you might think that's neither here nor there, and maybe you're right and maybe you're wrong, in any case, lean back in your seat a moment and listen to the tale. One morning, after they had heard the message, the two brothers went out to kill the boar. After they had eaten their breakfast, Karl took a two-handed sword and went off one way into the wild woods. Fritz took a bow and a quiverful of arrows and went into the wild woods another way. And about noon, when the sun was at its highest, and when all the little birds were quiet, Fritz heard a thrashing in the forest, and he saw the bushes trembling, and, because he thought that it was the savage boar coming to kill him, he whipped an arrow from his quiver and notched it in his bow and aimed it, but, instead of the dreadful boar, out of the bushes came a tiny little man carrying a black lance.

Fritz dropped his bow an inch or two, although not too far down, and stared at the tiny man, and the tiny man stared right back at him.

'Now then, Fritz,' said the midget. 'Just you take your finger off that bowstring there. Thank you. Now, because you are such a good-hearted lad, I am going to give you this black lance—' and he stabbed it into the ground. 'Take it,' he said, 'and have no fear. With this lance you will kill the terrible boar and then you will marry the Princess. Yes, don't be surprised, remember what the Good Book says: "Blest are the pure in heart."' Then he gave Fritz the lance and dived away into the heart of the thicket.

Fritz took the lance and struggled into the heart of the forest. Before long, he heard a terrible snorting and grunting and from the blackness of the trees came the boar, its little eyes red with rage and with froth swinging from its tusks. Fritz felt like climbing up the nearest tree but, like the brave lad he was, he stood his ground, and as the boar charged him he rammed the black lance into its breast. Then the boar grunted three times and fell down dead. Fritz wiped his forehead, and, although his hands were trembling, he tied the boar's legs together and dragged the beast back to his home.

Karl was in the house. He had gone home early because he had been afraid of meeting the boar. To try and forget his cowardice he had been drinking all afternoon and, in fact, he was drunk. When he saw Fritz coming with the boar he was bitterly jealous, but he was so sly and cunning that he hid his jealousy. 'Wonderful,' he said when Fritz got to the door. 'How wonderful that you have killed the savage boar. Come in and rest and drink some wine. You must be very tired.'

Because he was so pure-hearted, Fritz did not see that his brother was mad with envy, and so he went into the cottage and showed Karl the black lance and told him of the little man, and of how he had killed the boar, and together they celebrated the day's events.

Towards evening Fritz set off for the city, to show the King the boar and to claim his reward. He set off, dragging the boar behind him, but Karl followed him; and when they came to a bridge over a brook, Karl sprang on Fritz and hit him on the head with a club and killed him. Then Karl buried Fritz underneath the bridge, in the mud of the bed of the brook. After that he took the boar to the palace, told the King that he himself had killed the boar, married the Princess and, as they say, lived like a lord.

But evil deeds do not lie hidden in the dark for ever. In the long run they will be found out, one way or another, as you will hear.

Seven years passed and then, one day, a young shepherd lad was crossing the bridge. He leaned over the parapet to see if there were any fish in the river and saw, sticking from the mud, a little bone, washed as white as snow by the waters of the brook.

'Ah,' said the lad, 'a little bone. That is just what I need to make a mouthpiece for my flute.'

He waded into the brook, took the bone, carved it into a mouthpiece, and placed it on his flute. Then he sat upon the parapet and swung his legs and blew down the flute. But instead of playing a simple shepherd's song, the flute sang! Yes, it sang a quiet song, as sad as the sound of the wind in the reeds:

> 'Ah, little shepherd boy,
> You blow upon my knuckle bone.
> My own brother slaughtered me
> And buried me beneath the bridge
> So that he could take the boar
> And marry the King's daughter.'

The shepherd lad ran off to the King's palace and played his flute again, and again the flute sang its sad song. When the King heard it he went to the bridge with his soldiers and they found the skeleton of poor Fritz. The brother was dragged from the castle and when he saw the skeleton and heard the flute sing he confessed to the murder, and then the King had a millstone tied to his neck and had him thrown into the brook so that he drowned and paid for his wickedness. Then, by order of the King, Fritz's skeleton was taken to the cathedral and laid in a grave. And there, with a guardian angel at his head, he sleeps in peace until the Judgement Day.

The Golden Goose

A sausage maker had three sons. The youngest was quiet and shy and liked to go walking by himself in the countryside, looking at flowers and birds. Because of this people called him 'Dummling', which means 'stupid', and they jeered at him as though he was a freak.

One day the sausage maker's eldest son had to go into the forest to cut wood. For his lunch his mother gave him a plum cake and a bottle of good wine. He went into the forest but, before starting work, he sat down to have his lunch. While he was eating he saw a little grey-haired man watching him from the bushes.

'What are you staring at?' the eldest son said, rudely.

The little man came forward. 'Sorry,' he said. 'Only I haven't eaten for days and I wondered if you could spare me a bit of that cake.'

'What?' the eldest son said. 'If I give you some of my food I shall have less for myself. Go on, clear off before I give you a black eye.'

The little man shrugged and walked off into the forest. When he had gone, the eldest son picked up his axe and swung it at a tree, but the axe bounced back and cut his leg so badly that he had to dash home before he bled to death.

The next day the second son went into the forest to get the wood. For his lunch his mother gave him a big cherry cake and a bottle of beer. He went into the forest and he, too, decided to eat before he started work. As he was eating, the little man came from the bushes and asked for a piece of cake.

'Push off,' the second son said. 'What I give you I will have to take from myself. Go on, get going and find a job for yourself.'

'All right,' said the little man. 'Don't lose your hair,' and he walked away into the forest.

When he had gone, the second son picked up his axe and chopped at a tree; but the axe bounced back and hit him on the head and nearly knocked his brains out, so that he had to be carried home on a stretcher.

The next day Dummling said to his father, 'Dad, let me go and cut the wood.'

His father stared at him then burst out laughing. 'You!' he said. 'You! You cut wood? You are so stupid you couldn't even find the forest. No, no. Your brothers have hurt themselves, you would probably kill yourself. Leave well alone.'

But Dummling would not take no for an answer. He followed his father about the sausage factory asking to be allowed to cut the wood and in the end his father said:

'All right! All right then! Go and cut the wood and if you hurt yourself don't blame me.'

Dummling took the axe and his mother gave him some lunch, although all he got was a cinder-cake and a bottle of water. But Dummling did not complain. He swung the axe over his shoulder, picked up his lunch, and went off into the forest. When he got there he sat down to eat and the little man came and asked for food.

'Yes, of course,' Dummling said. 'I have only got cinder-cake and water but you are welcome to share it. I wouldn't see a man go short.'

The little man sat down next to Dummling, and when Dummling opened his parcel he found, instead of the cinder-cake and water, a steak and kidney pie and a bottle of champagne!

They ate and drank and when they had finished the little man said, 'Thank you, Dummling. You have a good heart so I will bring you good luck. Do you see that old tree over there?'

Dummling looked up and saw a gnarled old holly tree.

'Well,' said the man, 'cut that tree down and you will find something in its roots that you will like.' Then he ambled off into the forest.

Dummling chopped at the tree and his axe went through it like butter. After only one stroke the tree fell to the ground and in its roots Dummling saw a goose with golden feathers!

Dummling could not believe his eyes, but when he picked up the goose he realized that it was true. Every feather on the goose was purest gold.

'My word,' Dummling said, 'this is my lucky day.' He tucked the goose under his arm and walked from the forest but as he walked off he thought, Why should I go home? My brothers will only take the goose from me and my father will shout at me and call me stupid. No, I have the goose so that I will never go hungry, so I will go into the world and see what happens to me.

Dummling walked through the fields and in the evening he came to an inn where he decided to spend the night. He took a room, put the goose on the bed, then went out for a drink.

Now the innkeeper had three daughters and they had seen the golden goose. When Dummling went out the eldest daughter thought, What a marvellous bird. I will sneak into his room and steal a feather. No one will ever know.

She crept up the stairs into Dummling's room and tiptoed to the bed. 'Just one feather,' she said. 'One tiny feather,' and she plucked at the goose's tail. But the feather did not come out. Instead the goose turned its head and hissed and when the girl tried to take her hand away she found that she was stuck to the feather!

A minute or two later the second daughter crept into the room because she, too, thought that she would like a feather but she touched her sister, the goose hissed, and she found that she was stuck fast, as well!

The two girls stood together crying, and then the door opened and in came the third sister who saw no reason why she should not have a feather, also. As she entered the room her sisters shouted, 'Keep away. Clear off.'

The girl tossed her head. 'Pooh,' she cried. 'If you are going to have a feather then so shall I.'

She touched her sister, the goose hissed, and she was stuck, too! So the three of them had to spend the night with the goose.

The next morning Dummling put the goose under his arm and set off to see what the world had to offer. The three girls who were stuck to the goose had to follow him, and it was not a pleasant morning for them. Everywhere Dummling went they had to follow: left, right, up hill and down dale, into ditches and duckponds, through hedges and over stiles, and, try as they might they could not pull themselves free.

After a while, as they were crossing a field, they met a parson. When he saw them he went red in the face and his eyes bulged like a frog's.

'What are you doing?' he shouted. 'Stop it! Stop it! How dare you girls chase a young man like that. Stop it, you barefaced hussies.'

He grabbed at the youngest girl, the goose hissed, and he found that he was stuck fast with the others! Dummling ran on and the girls, and the parson, had to run on with him. Before long they came across a bishop who was coming from a big dinner. His face went purple.

'Good gracious me!' he cried. 'Parson, what on earth do you think that you are doing? You will make the church a laughing stock. Stop it at once.' He took hold of the parson's sleeve, the goose hissed, he was stuck fast, and, although he was fat and full of roast beef, he had to run with the rest of them.

On went Dummling, and on behind him went the three sisters, the parson, and the bishop. In the middle of the morning they came upon a workman digging up the road.

'Help,' called the bishop. 'Pull us free.'

The workman threw down his spade and pulled at the bishop. 'Hiss' went the goose and away went the workman. He had a sausage for his lunch stuck in his back pocket and as he ran along the sausage hung out. A hungry dog was sitting on the high road and as Dummling, and the three girls, and the parson, and the bishop, and the workman jogged past, it jumped up at the sausage but the goose hissed and it, too, was stuck.

As the church clocks struck twelve, they came to a city. The King of the city had a daughter who was so sad that she had never laughed. The King was so worried that he had said that whoever could make her laugh could marry her and be a prince. Many people had tried: comedians, clowns, jugglers and tumblers, although none had ever succeeded. But when the Princess saw Dummling run past the palace with the goose under his arm and, stuck to it, three girls, a thin parson, a fat bishop, a workman, and a dog biting a sausage, she burst out laughing and she shook until her sides ached.

Dummling laughed, too, but the King had a sour face. This Dummling isn't the man to marry my daughter, he thought. He looks like a half-wit. So when Dummling asked for the Princess's hand in marriage he made an excuse and said that first Dummling would have to find a man who could drink a whole cellarful of wine.

Dummling was not too happy about that, and who can blame him? Why, he thought, I might as well go home straight away. An elephant couldn't drink a cellarful of wine, let alone a man. But then he thought of the little man in the forest. 'He might help me,' he said to himself. 'Anyway, it's worth a try.'

Off he went to the forest and at the holly tree he came upon a man. The man was sitting on a tree stump and his face was so miserable it would have turned the milk sour. Dummling asked the man what was wrong.

'Thirst!' said the man. 'Horrible thirst. I am thirsty. I am always thirsty. But I can't stand water and a whole barrel of beer is no more to me than a raindrop on a hot stove.'

Dummling smiled and crooked his finger. 'Come with me, friend. Your troubles are over.'

He took the man to the King's cellar and the man lay under the taps of the gigantic barrels and drank until he was swollen like a balloon and all the barrels were empty.

Afterwards, Dummling went to the King and asked for his reward but still the King was not happy. If this man becomes my son-in-law every other king in the world will laugh at me, he thought. He sucked on his sceptre for a moment then he said:

'Dummling, before you marry my daughter you must find a man who can eat all the bread in the city.'

Dummling scratched his head. 'That's a tall order,' he said. 'An army couldn't do that.' But he was not down-hearted. He went to the forest to ask the little man if he would help.

By the holly tree, sitting on the same stump, he found another man. The man was pulling a terrible face and moaning and groaning and he was strapping a thick leather belt around his stomach.

'What is the matter?' Dummling asked.

'Hunger!' the man shouted. 'I am always hungry. I have just eaten ten sacks of potatoes and I am still starving. That is why I am strapping my stomach up, to stop the hunger pangs.'

Dummling raised his hands in the air. 'Sigh no more, friend,' he said. 'Just follow me.'

He took the man to the city and the man ran in and out of the shops gobbling up all the bread, and all the meat pies too, until there was not a crumb left.

Dummling paid the shopkeepers with feathers from the golden goose then went to the King and asked for the Princess, but the King made a third condition. He told Dummling that he must bring a ship which sailed on land

and sea. That will fix him, the King thought. No one can find such a ship because it does not exist and when Dummling comes back without one I'll kick him right out of my Kingdom. And I will keep the golden goose.

Dummling whistled when he heard the King's demand. 'A ship which sails on land and sea? I've never heard of such a thing, and I'll bet the King hasn't either. Still, let's see what can be done.'

Away he went to the forest, only this time he found the little man himself sitting on the tree stump. When he heard Dummling's request he whistled, too.

'Well, my friend,' he said. 'That *is* a tall order. Still, you were kind to me and I don't forget a kindness. You will have your ship.' Then he vanished down a rabbit hole.

Dummling left the forest and saw a ship in a field. He climbed aboard and the ship sailed across the field, down the river to the city, up the main street and into the palace yard. Then the King could not prevent the wedding any longer.

The next week all the church bells rang as Dummling and the Princess were married. The two of them were very happy, and they did a lot of bird watching together. When the King died, Dummling became King in his place and, although he did not say much, he ruled wisely and well for many a long year. And if you ever go to the city he ruled, you can still see Dummling's coat of arms on the palace gate. It is a little man sitting on a golden goose and underneath is Dummling's motto: 'Mercy, Pity, Peace, and Love'.

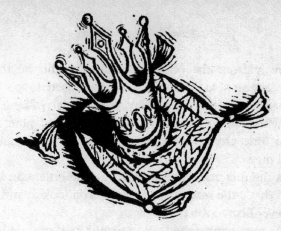

The King of the
Golden Mountain

There was once a merchant who had a son called Conrad. The child was still only an infant and had not yet learned to walk.

The merchant owned two ships and, one day, he had them laden with everything he possessed and sent to India because he thought that he would make a huge profit and become even richer than he was.

The merchant was happy at the thought of all the money he was going to make and he walked about the town in a jovial mood.

Then, after the ships had been at sea for three months, he got news which wiped the smile off his face. His ships had been captured by pirates and he would never see them again.

And so, instead of being a rich man, the merchant became a poor man, and now he walked about the town with a face as long as a fiddle.

The merchant had one thing left to him, a small field outside the town. To try and forget his problems, and to get away from the other townspeople who he thought were laughing at him, the merchant used to go to his field and walk there. One day, as he was walking about the field looking at a few cabbages he had planted, he saw a little green man sitting on a stone and smoking a straw pipe.

As the merchant approached him the little man looked up. 'What's the matter?' he asked. 'You look as miserable as Clever Elsa in the story.'

The merchant sighed. 'You would look miserable, too, if you were me.'

'What's the problem?' asked the green man.

The merchant shrugged. 'I would tell you if I thought you could help.'

The little man puffed on his tiny pipe. 'Maybe I can, maybe I can't. Who knows? But I certainly can't help if I don't know what your problem is.'

'All right.' The merchant sat down by the little man and told him what had happened to his ships.

'Well, now,' said the dwarf. 'I can help you there.'

'Can you?' asked the merchant, and for the first time in months he felt a flicker of hope.

'Sure,' said the dwarf. 'If it's only money you want that's no problem, none at all. I'll give you all the gold you want. But there is one condition.'

'I thought that there would be,' said the merchant. 'What is it?'

'Nothing at all, really,' the little man said. 'It is just this. Twelve years from now you must come back to this field and you must bring me a present.'

'What sort of a present?' asked the merchant.

'Well now,' the little man peered at the merchant over the bowl of his pipe. 'Let's say this. Let's say that you will bring me the first thing that rubs against your leg when you get home today. How's that?'

'That's fine,' said the merchant and he grinned behind his hand because he thought that the first thing which would rub against his leg when he got home would be his dog.

The big man and the tiny man shook hands on the bargain and then the merchant went home. But as he went into his house, instead of his dog, the first thing which brushed against his leg was his son, Conrad, who was crawling about the floor.

The man was frightened when Conrad brushed against his leg but, as a week or so passed and no money appeared, he thought that the little man had been playing a joke on him and so he would not have to lose his son. But then, one day, he went to his field to dig up his cabbages and underneath them he found a great heap of gold and silver.

Now the man became a rich merchant again, richer than ever before. He was not happy and jovial, though, but walked around with a long face, hiding his secret in his breast.

Twelve years passed away and Conrad grew up into a clever, sensible lad. He noticed how miserable his father looked and one day he asked him what was the matter.

The father sighed. Tears trickled down his care-worn cheeks as he told Conrad that the day had nearly arrived when he must be given to the little green man.

But Conrad smiled and took his father's hand. 'Don't worry, father,' he said. 'That dwarf won't have me. Just you wait and see.'

The day came when the twelve years were up. That morning Conrad went to the priest to be blessed and in the afternoon he went to the field to meet the dwarf. When they got there Conrad drew a circle in the soil and inside the circle he scratched a star then he took his father by the hand and stood inside the circle.

A little time passed and then, as the church clock chimed three, the little green man came hurrying across the field rubbing his hands together and smoking his little straw pipe. But when he saw the magic circle he stopped and scowled.

'What is this?' he said. 'Why are you drawing magic circles? Hand over the boy.'

The father could not bring himself to speak but Conrad spoke up boldly. 'What do you want?' he cried.

'Shut up, you,' squeaked the little man. 'I came here to speak to your father.'

'Well you will have to speak to me instead,' said Conrad.

The dwarf stamped his feet with rage but he could not cross the magic circle. 'I kept my part of the bargain,' he said. 'Now your father must keep his.'

Conrad shook his head. 'You tricked my father,' he said.

'No,' said the dwarf. 'I will not give up my rights. I won't.'

Conrad and the dwarf argued and bickered but neither would give way. At last they came to an agreement. As Conrad would not agree that he belonged to the dwarf, and the dwarf would not agree that the lad still belonged to his father, they decided that he belonged to no one and should be cast adrift on the ocean in an open boat and that fate and destiny should deal with him.

They went to the sea-shore and Conrad said goodbye to his father and clambered into an open boat and the father pushed him off, wading thigh deep in the water so that he might be with his son as long as possible. But before the boat had gone very far a wave struck it and overturned it. The father ran along the shore shouting to his son but there was neither sight nor sound of Conrad. The father thought that his son was drowned and he went home full of grief.

But although the boat had overturned Conrad had managed to keep hold of the seat and, although his body was in the water, his head was above it although covered by the boat.

The wind and the waves took the boat across the sea until it grounded on an island. Conrad climbed from under the boat and saw, on a mountain, a castle whose turrets and towers were topped with gold. He hurried up the mountain but, although the castle was large and magnificent, there was not one soldier or courtier in it.

Conrad looked in every room, but not even a mouse stirred or spider spun. And then, in the very last room, he found a snake, striped black and yellow, coiled in a ring on the floor. Conrad lifted up a chair to kill the snake but, as he lifted the chair, the snake uncoiled itself and turned into a beautiful girl.

'Ah,' said the girl. 'At last you have come! For twelve years I have lain under a spell waiting for you. Now you can free me and all this Kingdom of the Golden Mountain from the spell.'

'How can I do that?' Conrad asked.

'You must do this,' the Princess said. 'Tonight twelve demons will come here. They will ask what you are doing here, but you must not answer them. They will torment you; they will beat you and burn you but you must not speak. At the stroke of midnight they will have to go back into Hell. Tomorrow night twenty-four demons will come and torment you, and on the next night thirty-six demons will come. They will torture you and at midnight they will cut off your head. But if you do not speak, if you do not utter one word or sound, then I will be saved. And when I am saved I will come with a magic salve which has the breath of life in it and make you whole again. Will you do this for me?'

'I will,' said Conrad, and the girl changed back into a snake and coiled herself in a ring on the cold, marble floor.

As the girl had said, so it happened. First twelve demons came and tortured Conrad, but he did not speak. The next night twenty-four demons tortured him, and on the third night thirty-six demons tormented him and, as he remained silent, at midnight they chopped off his head and returned to Hell. But as they vanished, the snake uncoiled its black and yellow body and turned into the princess and she took the salve of life to Conrad and cured him. Then the spell on the castle was broken. The princess married Conrad and he became the King of the Golden Mountain.

Conrad and his wife lived together in great happiness and, in time, they had a son. But after nine years Conrad began to think of his father and his heart was so touched that he wanted to visit him again. But when he said that he was going to leave the Kingdom his Queen would not hear of it.

'You will never return,' she said.

'I will return,' Conrad said. 'I will return although the Devil himself tries to stop me.' And he spoke so often of his desire to see his father that in the end the Queen said that he could go.

'Go, then,' she said, 'although I know evil will come of this. But take this ring and wear it on your finger. It is a wishing ring and wherever you wish to go to, the ring will take you. But you must promise me one thing. Whatever happens you must never wish that I should leave this Kingdom.'

Conrad promised, put the wishing ring on his finger, and wished that he was back in Germany. The sky went dark, there was a huge crack of lightning, and when Conrad opened his eyes he found that he was standing before the gates of his home town. He tried to go through the gates but his clothes were so strange that the guard would not let him enter the town.

Conrad offered the guard money but was told to clear off, and so he went away and wandered here and there until, on a hill, he met a shepherd. He and the shepherd exchanged their clothes, and, dressed in the shepherd's rough smock, Conrad went back to the town. This time the guard let him in and soon he was at his father's house.

He knocked at the door and asked if he could have water to drink. A servant took him into the house and Conrad's father, from the goodness of his heart, and because he thought that the visitor was merely a poor shepherd, gave the guest food and drink.

While he was eating, Conrad asked his mother and father if they had ever had a son.

The father looked sad. 'Yes,' he answered. 'We had a son, but we lost him many years ago.'

Conrad put down his spoon. 'Now be sad no longer,' he said. 'For I am your son!'

Conrad expected that his father and mother would fall on his neck and kiss him but, instead, they looked angry.

'We don't want any tricks,' they said. 'Many a man comes here and says that, because they want to inherit our money. Be off or we will set the dogs on you.'

Conrad smiled. 'Tell me,' he said. 'Did your son have any mark on him which you would recognize?'

'Yes,' said the mother. 'On his arm he had a mark like a moth.'

Conrad rolled up his shirt sleeve. 'Look,' he said, and there on his arm was a birthmark like a tiny moth.

The mother put her hand to her breast. 'It is my son,' she cried. 'It is my son,' and she took Conrad in her arms and wept.

The father opened a bottle of wine and they drank to the return of Conrad.

'But where have you been all these years?' the father asked.

'Ah!' Conrad smiled and told his parents that he was a king, the King of the Golden Mountain, and that he had a queen for his wife and that they had a fine child of seven years old.

When he had finished his tale his father half-hid a smile. 'Yes,' he said, 'that is a fine tale, my son, but there is no need to tell a romance. We love you for yourself and for yourself alone.'

Conrad was angry. 'What do you mean?' he demanded.

The father shrugged. 'Why, nothing,' he said. 'But how can you be a king when you are dressed like an old, ragged shepherd? No, no. But it is of no consequence to us. I tell you, we love you because you are our own son who we thought had been lost to us for ever.'

Conrad grew angrier. Twice more he told his tale and twice more his father smiled and shook his head and patted him on the shoulder. Then Conrad stood up.

'All right,' he shouted, 'I will prove it to you!' And without thinking he twisted the wishing ring on his finger and cried, 'Let my wife and child come here!'

There was a tremendous crash of thunder, the sky went black, and when it grew light again the Queen and the child were standing in the room!

'Ah,' cried the Queen. 'Conrad, you have deceived me. You promised that you would never wish me away from my own country.'

Conrad took her hand. 'Forgive me,' he said. 'Please forgive me. I did it without thinking.'

The Queen wept but, after a little while, she stopped crying and Conrad thought that she had forgiven him.

'Good,' Conrad said. 'Now let me take you to where I was cast off in a boat and began my adventures which led me to you.'

He took the Queen to the shore and, after a while, he fell asleep on the Queen's lap. When he was sleeping soundly the Queen carefully drew her legs away from under his head, and then she took the wishing ring from his finger.

'Now,' she said, 'false-heart, live as you were born, for you will be King of the Golden Mountain no longer!' And she wished herself and her child away to her own country; but, as she vanished, she left behind her slipper which was caught under Conrad's arm.

The tide coming in splashed on Conrad's foot and woke him, and he saw that he was alone on the bleak sea-shore and when he saw that the wishing ring was gone from his finger he knew that his wife and child had left him. For a while he sat on the rocks and wept from sorrow and grief, and when his tears had dried he sat for longer, his hand on his chin, staring out at the grey waters of the sea.

At last he stood up. Home I can't go, he thought. For the people of the town would demand to see my wife and child and they might put me to death for murder and for being a wizard. But I will find my way to my Kingdom of the Golden Mountain if it takes me the rest of my life.

He set off walking and at the end of the day he came to a hill. Three giants were standing on the hill, arguing. When they saw Conrad they called to him to join them. Conrad was afraid, because he had heard that giants ate ordinary men for a snack, but the eldest giant told him not to be afraid.

'It's like this,' the giant said. 'We are brothers. Our father died last week and left us his property and since then we have been standing here arguing about how to divide it. Now, little men have quick wits, as they say, so we want you to divide the property fairly.'

'Very well,' said Conrad. 'What is the property?'

The giant pointed and there on the ground were a sword, a cloak, and a pair of boots.

Conrad shrugged his shoulders. 'Why,' he said, 'they are not worth arguing over.'

'No,' said the giant. 'You don't understand. These are magic things. If you wear the cloak you become invisible. The boots will take you anywhere you wish, and if you hold the sword and say, "All heads off but mine," everyone's head will fall off but your own.'

'I see,' said Conrad. 'Well, let me try them, so that I can be sure that they are in good condition. Give me the cloak first.'

The giants shook their heads. 'No, no,' they said. 'If you put on the cloak you might run away and we could not see you to follow you.'

'All right,' said Conrad, 'then carry on arguing.' And he made to walk away, but the giants stopped him and gave him the cloak. Conrad tried it on and at once became invisible. The giants looked anxious but Conrad slipped the cloak off and became visible, which cheered the giants up a little!

'Now let me try the sword,' Conrad said.

The youngest giant felt his neck. 'I don't know about that,' he said. 'You might cut our heads off.'

The other giants felt their necks, too, but in the end they gave Conrad the sword although they said that he must only use it on a tree. Conrad took the sword and swung it against a mighty oak tree and the sword went through the trunk as if it were made of butter.

'Good,' Conrad said. 'That is a good sword. Now let me try the boots.'

Again the giants shook their heads. 'If you wear the boots,' they said, 'you could wish yourself anywhere in the world and we would have lost them.'

'I won't do that,' Conrad said. 'I am an honest fellow.' And so the giants gave him the boots.

Conrad put them on, and slung the cloak over his shoulders, and took the sword, and, although he had given his word to the giants, yet, invisible and all powerful as he was, he could think only of his wife and child and his Kingdom of the Golden Mountain, and, almost as though it was another person speaking, his mouth opened and he cried: 'Take me to the Golden Mountain!' and he soared away leaving the giants looking sorrowfully at each other.

In three strides of the magic boots Conrad was back in his Kingdom. He took the cloak from his shoulders and strode to his palace. It was growing dark but light was streaming from every window, and there was the sound of music and laughter. Conrad stopped a swineherd and asked him what the music was for.

'Why,' said the lad, 'it is for our Queen. Her husband, the King, betrayed her and deserted her, but now he is dead and the Queen is marrying another prince.'

When Conrad heard that, his heart felt as though it had turned into a slab of ice. 'I betrayed her?' he cried. 'It was she, that false woman, who tricked and betrayed me, and deserted me while I was asleep. And now she would marry another! Well, we will see what we will see.'

He put the magic cloak on and strode into the palace, invisible and unseen. In the great banqueting hall, at the head of a table covered with food and wine, sat the Queen, dressed in a magnificent purple gown and with the royal crown on her head. And beside her, dressed in scarlet and silver was the prince she wished to marry.

Conrad prowled down the banqueting hall and stood behind the Queen. When she put a piece of meat on her plate, Conrad took it away and ate it, and when she had wine poured into her glass Conrad took that and drank it. No matter what the Queen took, Conrad took it also, so that, although the guests were well fed and merry, the Queen was hungry and sad.

The Queen was ashamed and ran to her chamber but Conrad followed her there. The Queen stood before the fire weeping. 'Has the Devil power over me?' she cried. 'Am I yet as I was seven years ago? Did my deliverer never come?'

Then Conrad struck the Queen in the face. 'Did your deliverer never come?' he shouted. 'Yes, he came, and for three nights he endured the torture of the demons to deliver you. And he has come again, only now it is he who has you in his power. Oh, traitor, did I deserve this from you?'

Conrad took off his cloak and made himself visible as the Queen wept and wrung her hands. He marched into the banqueting hall and swept the dishes from the table with his sword, and cried, 'The wedding feast is over, the true King has returned. Begone, all of you!'

But the guests refused to leave. They laughed at Conrad and ridiculed him, and the Prince in scarlet and silver threw a glass of wine at him. Once more Conrad struck the table. 'Will you go or not?' he cried.

Then the guests were angry. They took out their swords and ran at Conrad. He shouted, 'Beware, beware, beware,' three times, but as they would not heed him he swung his sword and cried—'All heads off but mine!'

And all the heads of all his subjects fell off and rolled on the ground; and, in her chamber, the Queen's head fell off too; and Conrad alone was Master, and he alone was King, and he alone was Ruler, yes, and he was alone on the Golden Mountain.

The Queen Bee

Before you were born, and before your parents were
born, and before your grandparents were born,
and before their grandparents were born, and
before their great, great, great, great, great grandparents
were born, there was a king who had three sons. The two
eldest sons were terrible wild lads and, although, or
perhaps because, they had been given everything they
ever asked for, they were greedy, mean, spiteful, and
cruel.

Although the King needed their help in ruling his land,
his sons wandered away and lived such wicked, wasteful
lives, drinking and gambling, that they did not return
home again.

The King was sad with such a deep sadness that the
youngest son, who everyone called Simpleton because he
was a modest and kind lad, decided that he would go into
the world and find his two brothers and bring them back
to his father, the King.

Simpleton was mocked when he set out into the world.
When they saw him ride out the people grinned like
donkeys. 'That Simpleton will never find his brothers,'

they brayed. 'He couldn't find his hat if it wasn't on his head. Hee hee, haw, haw, haw.'

Simpleton paid no attention and in fact, after much wandering here and there, he found his brothers in a tavern at the world's end. Just like everyone else they sneered at him and when he said that their father was sad they laughed in Simpleton's face.

'What is that to us?' they shouted. 'Let him die of grief if he wants to. We are going to enjoy ourselves while we are young.'

The two older brothers left the inn and wandered into a faraway land, but Simpleton followed them every inch of the way. After a while, as they were crossing a field, they found an ant hill. The two brothers wanted to destroy the ant hill so that they could laugh as the little ants crept about in terror trying to save their eggs. They got sticks to knock the ant hill down but Simpleton stopped them.

'Leave the poor creatures alone,' he said. 'What harm have they done you?'

And although he was a simpleton he was strong and so he stopped his brothers.

A little later they came to a stream. On the stream were a duck and a drake and a brood of ducklings, living a quiet life under the cool, green shade of the willows.

'Aha!' cried the brothers. 'Let's kill the ducklings. The drake and the duck will quack with grief. It will be very funny.'

Simpleton was angry. 'Kill those ducklings and I will kill you,' he said. 'The little creatures will swim safely while I am here.'

The brothers were angry but they were afraid of Simpleton and so they slouched off, muttering to themselves.

They left the stream and came to a wood. In the wood there was a tree with a bees' nest in it. The nest was so full of honey that it was oozing from the hollow in the tree. The two brothers wanted to make a fire and kill the bees so that they could eat all the honey, but once again Simpleton stopped them.

'The honey is for the baby bees,' he said. 'Let the little things live. They have their lives to live as well as you.'

Once again the brothers had to give up because they knew that Simpleton would knock them down if they tried to kill the bees.

That evening the three brothers left the wood and came upon a castle. They walked through the courtyard and saw soldiers, but every one of them was made of stone. They peered into the stables but all that was there were stone horses and stone grooms. In the castle itself there were stone servants and stone dogs and, in the stateroom, there was a stone king and a stone queen and stone courtiers, and even a stone ambassador. The brothers went upstairs by a stone staircase. They went through all the rooms and found nothing but stone beds and chairs. But at the end of a corridor they found a door with three locks. In the door there was a hole and through the hole they saw a man sitting at a stone table.

The brothers called to the man but he did not hear. They called again but he did not answer. But the third time they called he turned, slowly, and looked at them. For a second or two he remained sitting and then he rose and walked towards the door with a curious slow, stiff walk. As he reached the brothers they saw that his face was grey and rigid and his eyes were blank, like a statue.

The man did not say a word but took the brothers into a dining-room. The table was laid with superb food but all of it was made of stone. The brothers shook their heads and then the man led them each to a bedroom where, although they slept, none of them was comfortable because the pillows and sheets were made of stone, too!

The next morning the man took the eldest brother into a graveyard. On a tombstone there were three sentences carved, and this was the first, which the eldest brother read:

'Hidden under the moss in the forest there are one thousand pearls. If they are found then the spell on this palace will be broken and the finder will marry the daughter of the King. But if all the pearls are not found by sunset then the seeker will be turned into stone also.'

The eldest brother ran off to the forest and searched for the pearls, but when sunset came he had only found one hundred and he was turned into stone.

The next day the second brother tried his luck but he found two hundred only and when the sun set he, too, was turned into stone.

The third day it was Simpleton's turn. He went into the forest and searched through the moss but as sunset drew near he had only found three hundred pearls. The sun slipped closer and closer to the horizon and Simpleton was in despair. He sat on a log and held his head in his hands and stared at the grim shapes of his brothers. But as he sat there he heard a rustling noise, a creeping and stirring in the forest floor and looking down he saw a million ants running through the moss led by the King of the Ants whose people Simpleton had saved from his

brothers' cruelty! The ants ran about the moss and before
the sun had set they had found every one of the thousand
hidden pearls and given them to Simpleton.

Simpleton went to the palace and gave the pearls to
the grey man, but the next morning the man led him to
the graveyard and pointed to the tombstone again. The
next sentence said:

> 'Three Princesses lie in their chamber. The
> key to the chamber is at the bottom of the
> largest lake in the kingdom. Unless the key is
> found the Princesses will be locked away for
> ever.'

Simpleton ran to the lake and dived in. But the bed of
the lake was so choked with weed and clogged with mud
that the lad knew that he could never find the key. But just
as he was about to despair he heard a quack-quack-
quacking and the beating of many wings and down on the
lake landed a thousand ducks, led by the Queen of the
Ducks, who had not forgotten that Simpleton had saved
the little ducklings.

The ducks landed on the lake and turned their bottoms
up and before the sun had set they had found the key
and given it to Simpleton. He went to the palace and gave
it to the grey man, but Simpleton's tasks were not over
yet. The next morning he was taken to the graveyard and
shown the third sentence, which said:

> 'The Princesses lie in their chamber. You
> must kiss the youngest and the prettiest. But
> if you choose wrongly then you, too, will be
> turned into stone.'

Simpleton ran to the Princesses' chamber and opened the door with the key. He thought that it would be easy to choose the youngest and the prettiest Princess, but what he found were three stone figures whose faces looked exactly alike.

Simpleton hovered first over one face, then another, but each time he bent forward to kiss the lips of the timeless masks he hesitated.

'Suppose I choose the wrong statue?' he wondered. 'Then I shall be turned into stone forever.'

The shadows crept across the room and still Simpleton could not decide what to do but, just as the sun was touching the hills, he heard a buzzing and through the window flew the Queen of the Bees, who had not forgotten that Simpleton had saved the hive from the greed of his brothers.

The Queen Bee hovered over the Princesses, for she knew what Simpleton did not know, which was this: before the three sisters had been turned into stone they had each taken a sweet. The oldest had taken sugar, the second had taken syrup, and the youngest and prettiest had taken honey.

The Queen Bee hovered over the Princess who had taken syrup, then she rose a little in the air and flew to the second princess. For a second or two she hovered there and then she flew to the third princess but she did not hover there. No, she landed on the lips and so Simpleton knew that was the Princess he must choose. He leaned forward and kissed the Princess and she, and the whole court, shattered their cold and stony frames and were restored to life.

So the story came to a happy end. At least it did for Simpleton for he married the pretty Princess and in time became a king in his own right. But as for the idle, wanton brothers, they each married the other two Princesses who soon became fat and ugly and who nagged their husbands all the rest of their days.

And when next you see a small and harmless creature, think of this tale. Do no harm but only good, and surely good will come to you.

The Three Little
Men in the Wood

O n the edge of the Black Forest there lived a man
whose wife died. Not far away there was a
woman whose husband had died. The man had a
daughter called Freda, and the woman had a daughter
called Elsa. Elsa and Freda used to meet at the village well
and they became friends.

One day, when they were playing at the widow's
cottage, the woman said, 'Freda, my dear, I want you to
give your father a message from me. Tell him I want to
marry him, and tell him that if he does wed me then I will
be a good wife to him and a good mother to you. Say that
if I become your stepmother then you will bathe in milk
and drink fine wine, but my own daughter will wash in
cold water and drink sour beer.'

The widow smiled and stroked Freda's hair and gave
her a cake. She knew how to worm her way into people's
hearts!

Freda went home and told her father what the widow
had said. The man stared into the fire.

'What shall I do?' he said. 'Marriage is a blessing and a curse. I need a wife and you need a mother, but still . . .'

The man could not make up his mind. All night he thought about it and the next morning he pulled off his boot and gave it to Freda.

'Here,' he said. 'Take this boot. It has a hole in the heel. Go into the yard and hang it on a nail and pour water into it. If the water stays in the boot I will marry the widow, if it runs out through the hole then I won't.'

Freda did as her father said but the water made the boot tip forward and so the water poured into the toe of the boot and did not run out through the hole in the heel. Freda told her father and he went to see for himself.

'That decides it,' he said, and he told the widow he would marry her.

Three weeks later, after the banns had been called, the man and the woman were married. The day after the wedding the two girls went into the kitchen and it was just as the widow had promised. By Freda's place there was milk for her to wash in and fine wine for her to drink, but at Elsa's place there was only cold water and sour beer.

The next morning the girls came down again and at Elsa's place there was cold water and wine, and at Freda's place there was milk and sour beer. The third day the girls came down and there at Elsa's place was milk and wine but at Freda's place there was cold water and sour beer!

And that is how the woman treated the two girls. She gave her own daughter all the juicy tit-bits off the meat while poor Freda had to make do with the fat and gristle, and Freda had to drudge away in the house while Elsa lay in bed until noon and then idled the day away, stuffing herself with cakes.

The man tried to protect his daughter, but if he spoke

for her the woman screamed and screeched and nagged him from dawn till dusk, until finally he gave up and spent all his time out of the house.

As the autumn passed away the woman began to hate Freda more and more, especially because, as the girls grew older, Freda became beautiful and kind, and Elsa became ugly and spiteful.

The winter came and a bitter winter it was. Hill and dale were deep in snow, and icicles as thick as a man's arm hung from every tree. One day the woman made a dress of paper and made Freda put it on. Then she gave her a basket and said:

'Go into the forest and bring me back some wild strawberries. It is a long time since I tasted any.'

'Wild strawberries?' cried Freda. 'Strawberries do not grow in winter, the earth is frozen as hard as iron. Besides, if I go out in a paper dress I shall die of the cold. The wind will blow through the dress and the thorns will tear it from me.'

'What?' shouted the woman. 'Do you dare to contradict me?' She slapped Freda across the face. 'Do as you are told. One more word from you and I will send you out without shoes on your feet. Get out, and don't come back without strawberries.'

She pushed Freda out through the door and threw a tiny piece of stale bread after her. 'Have that for your dinner,' she cried.

Then she sat by the fire with Elsa and had tea and toast and rubbed her hands together. 'That Freda will die of cold,' she said, 'and good riddance to her. Then we will have everything in the house for ourselves.'

Outside, Freda wandered through the snow into the forest. It was so cold that even the wolves stayed in their dens. The thorns ripped holes in Freda's dress and the wind blew through them, and she thought that she would freeze to death. But, just as she could go no further, she saw a tiny house and peeping at her through the window were three little men.

Freda tapped at the door and the men ran to open it. 'Come in,' they cried. 'Come and sit by the stove and get warm.'

Freda warmed her hands and then took out the scrap of stale bread she had been given for her lunch. The little men looked at the bread and one said:

'Child, we have no food in the house. Will you share your bread with us?'

'Yes indeed,' said Freda. 'There is little enough but what there is you are welcome to.'

She divided the bread and, although each had only a crumb, yet it seemed as if they were having a feast. As they sat eating the eldest little man leaned forward.

'Little one,' he asked, 'why are you wandering in the forest wearing only a paper dress?'

'I have been sent to find wild strawberries,' said Freda.

The little man was amazed. 'Strawberries? In winter?'

'Yes,' replied Freda, 'and I am not to go home without them.'

The three little men looked at each other and then the youngest said:

'Now, my dear, you have warmed yourself by our stove. Take the broom and sweep away the snow from our back door.'

Freda brushed the crumbs from her knees, took the broom, and went to the back door. When she was out of the room the eldest dwarf said:

'That is a fine girl. She has shared all she had with us, although she had little enough for herself, and she was ready to clean our back doorstep. We must give her a gift each. Mine is that she will grow more beautiful every day.'

'Yes,' said the second little man. 'And mine is that she will marry a king.'

'And mine,' said the third, 'is that every time she speaks a golden piece will fall from her lips.'

While the little men were talking Freda was sweeping the snow away from the back door. And under the snow she found ripe strawberries, glowing deep red. She gathered the fruit, kissed each of the little men, thanked them, and ran home.

As Freda entered her house she said, 'Good evening,' and a gold piece dropped from her lips! She told her stepmother and Elsa what had happened to her and with every word she spoke a gold piece fell from her lips.

As they heard the tale the mother and her daughter scowled and finally Elsa stamped on the floor.

'Just look at her!' she cried. 'Look at her arrogance! Sitting there and spilling money all over the floor. Get out. Go to bed, you cheeky cat.'

Freda went to her cot in the attic and Elsa glowered into the fire, her face as sour as a crab apple.

'Tomorrow I will go into the forest,' she said. 'Then I will come back with gold dropping from my lips.'

Her mother argued with her. She said that it was too cold for her precious darling. 'You will get chilblains,' she said.

But Elsa would not listen. 'I shall go,' she screamed. 'I shall, I shall, I shall!'

The next morning the mother muffled Elsa in a fur coat,

thick boots, a scarf, gloves, and a warm hat, and in a basket she put a huge pie, eggs, cake, and wine.

'And if you feel the teeniest bit cold,' she said, 'you must come back at once.'

Elsa plodded off to the forest although she had so many clothes on she could hardly walk. At length she came to the cottage and the three little men peered at her through the window. Elsa did not even bother to knock at the door but just charged in and, without so much as a 'by your leave', she sat by the stove and began to eat her lunch.

The little men watched her for a while and then the eldest man asked her if she could spare them some food.

'Pooh!' Elsa threw back her head. 'There is not enough food here for me, let alone you. Get your own food.' And she gobbled up the pie, four eggs, and a plum cake.

When she had finished the youngest man leaned forward. 'My dear,' he said, 'we are only little and the snow outside is deep. Will you sweep it away for us?'

Elsa stared at the little man as if he were a worm. 'What do you think I am?' she said. 'I am not a servant, sweep your own snow away. And don't call me your dear, either. I am a lady!'

She flounced out to look for strawberries and the three little men looked at each other.

'What a proud, spiteful creature,' said the eldest little man. 'We must give *her* a present, too. Mine is that she will grow more ugly every day.'

'Yes,' the middle little man agreed. 'And mine is that she will die a miserable death.'

The third little man nodded in agreement. 'And mine is that every time she speaks a toad will jump out of her nasty mouth.'

Elsa plodded around the house looking for strawberries but she found none. Without even saying goodbye to the little men she stalked home in a fine temper. When she got there she opened her mouth to complain but instead of words a toad jumped from her mouth.

From that day onward Elsa grew uglier and uglier and every time she spoke toads jumped from her mouth and everyone she met fled from her in horror. Even Elsa's own mother was horrified, but her hatred was turned on Freda, who grew more beautiful every day. Night after night the mother thought of a way to kill Freda and at last, as winter drew to an end, a plan came to her.

The next day she put a big pan on the fire and put linen thread in it and water. When the water had boiled she called to Freda.

'Take this pan to the river,' she snapped. 'I want you to rinse the thread clean. And mind that you go out into the middle of the river where the current is swift so that the thread gets washed properly.'

Freda put her hand to her mouth. 'But the ice on the river is thin,' she said. 'If I go to the middle the ice will break and I will fall into the water and drown.'

'Rubbish!' cried her stepmother. 'I have been across the river many times. Take an axe with you to cut a hole in the ice. Now go or I will throw this boiling water over you.'

Freda took the pan and went to the river and as she went her stepmother laughed because she was sure that the hot pan would melt the thin ice and that Freda would be drowned.

At the river Freda began to creep across the ice but before she had gone too far a carriage came rattling along the river bank, and in the carriage was a king.

The King saw the beautiful girl crossing the dangerous ice and he called to his coachman to halt and to bring the girl to him. The King asked Freda what she was doing on the river on such a bitter day. Freda told him and the King was so enchanted by her beauty that he asked her to marry him. Freda blushed but said that she would, and so she went away with the King and was married in great splendour, as the little men had promised.

After a year the new Queen had a son. The stepmother heard of this and her hatred and jealousy of Freda was worse than ever. She put on her best clothes and dressed Elsa in a new gown and a veil and went to the castle, pretending that she was on a friendly visit.

'Let bygones be bygones,' she said to Freda. 'I forgive all your nasty little ways!'

Freda merely smiled and said, 'Thank you,' which made the woman more bitter than ever.

'Never mind,' she hissed at Elsa. 'We will teach the minx a lesson. Who does she think she is to smile at me!'

Night and day the woman and Elsa lurked about the castle looking for a chance to do Queen Freda harm, but always the King was with her. One day, though, he had to go away to see another king and that night the woman and Elsa crept into the Queen's room, seized her by the head and the feet, and threw her through the window into the castle moat.

'That is the end of her,' cried the stepmother. 'And good riddance to bad rubbish.'

Then she shoved Elsa into the Queen's bed and told her to lie with the sheets over her head and not to say a word. At midnight the King returned and wanted to speak to his wife but the stepmother stopped him.

'No,' she said. 'The Queen has been tired and now she has gone to sleep. Leave her to rest.'

The King went to his own room but the next morning he went back and spoke to the girl he thought was his wife. Elsa answered him but, although she kept her veil over her face, every time she spoke a toad jumped from her mouth on to the counterpane.

The King was horrified but the stepmother took him aside and said:

'Last night the Queen was ill. It is nothing, and she will soon be better. These toads are just from the sweat of the sickness.'

The King was concerned, but he believed the stepmother, and he left the room and got on with his affairs while the stepmother and Elsa sat cackling in the bedroom.

But that evening a kitchen boy saw a duck swimming on the moat. The duck looked up and opened its yellow beak and quacked at the lad:

> 'Quack, quack, little kitchen lad,
> What is my King doing now,
> Does he sleep or does he wake?'

The kitchen lad was so astonished that he could not answer. Then the duck spoke again:

> 'Quack, quack, little kitchen lad,
> What are my guests doing now,
> Do they sleep or do they wake?'

The lad leaned over the battlement and answered:

'Little duck, little duck,
They are both sound asleep.'

The duck bobbed her head and asked:

'Quack, quack, little kitchen lad,
Where is my baby now,
Does he sleep or does he wake?'

The lad threw some crusts down to the duck and said:

'Little duck, little duck,
He is in his cradle, fast asleep.'

The duck paddled away but that night she flew from the moat to the nursery. She fed her baby, and made up the cradle, which the stepmother had not bothered to do, and then flew back to the moat. The next night she came again and did the same thing, but the third night she called to the kitchen lad and told him to fetch the King with his sword.

The King came and the duck told him to swing his sword over her head three times. The King took out his bright sword and swung it, and on the third swing the duck changed into Queen Freda!

The King and the Queen embraced, but Freda told the King to be silent until their son was baptized on the following Sunday. She hid in a cupboard until the day came while, for three days, the stepmother told the King that Elsa was his wife and she was still poorly and could not see him.

On the Sunday the child was given to Christ and afterwards, at the baptism party, the King called the stepmother and Elsa to him.

'I have a case in my court,' he said. 'Two villains threw an innocent woman into the river and drowned her. What punishment should I give?'

The stepmother drank some port wine. 'Why, there is only one punishment that the two wretches deserve,' she said. 'Put them in a barrel studded with great iron nails and roll the barrel down a hill into the river.'

'And should I show no mercy?' asked the King.

'Certainly not,' said the stepmother, and Elsa screeched, 'Certainly not,' as well.

'Very well,' said the King. 'You have sentenced yourselves.'

He ordered a barrel to be brought and nailed and he put the stepmother and Elsa in it and they were rolled down a hill into the river where they both drowned.

And so the words of the three little men came true. Freda married a King while Elsa died a horrible death. Freda asked the little men to live in the palace but they said that they were very happy in their house in the woods. As for the kitchen lad, the King made him a duke and he married the Queen's daughter and became a King in his turn. But, although he was a great King, he always called his Queen, his little duckling!

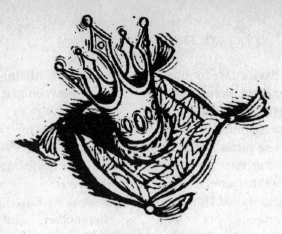

Cinderella

When old folk get together they often say, 'Hill and dale will never meet,' by which they mean, the rich and the poor will never come together. But they can be wrong, as this tale tells.

A rich man had a wife. After some years the wife fell ill. The doctors could not cure her and there came a day when she knew that she was dying. As her end drew near she called her only daughter to her.

'Dear child,' she said, 'we must part soon and we shall not meet again in this world. But be good and kind and God will protect you, and I will look down from Heaven and watch over you.' Then she closed her eyes and died.

Every day after that the daughter went to her mother's grave and wept, but she did her best to be good and kind, as her mother had told her to be.

The winter came and spread a white sheet over the grave, and by the time spring had drawn the sheet away, the girl's father had taken another wife.

The man's new wife had two daughters. Like their mother they were beautiful, but they were vain and haughty and greedy, and they hated their stepsister because she was modest, humble, and generous. That is how it is in life, the wicked envy the good and because of that envy they persecute the good.

And the two daughters persecuted their stepsister. 'Is she to sit with us in the parlour?' they whined. 'Turn her out. Let her sit in the scullery.' They took away her dresses and made her wear an old, grey gown and clogs. Having done that, they then mocked her. 'Look at the fine princess,' they screeched. 'What fine clothes she wears. Hee, hee, hee.' And, although neither of them ever did a hand's turn they said, 'If you do not work then you will not eat. Get into the kitchen and peel the potatoes.'

They turned the child into a drudge; she fetched and carried from morn till night, carrying water, making the fires, cooking and washing, and cleaning the house.

But even that was not enough for the two sisters. They tormented their stepsister by playing cruel tricks on her. After she had cleaned the floor they deliberately walked on it with muddy shoes, or they would kick the dustbin over so that the girl had to go on her hands and knees and clean up the mess.

They even refused to let her have a bed of her own so that at night, when she dropped with weariness, like the cat she had to sleep by the cinders in the kitchen hearth. There, each night, she lay and dreamed of her mother, and the tears rolled down her cheeks and streaked the ash dust on her face. The two sisters were cruel enough to laugh at that. 'You are like a cat,' they tittered. 'You are like a cat with stripes on its face, hee, hee, hee.' And because the girl had ash and cinders in her hair they called her 'Cinderella'.

One day the father was going to the fair and he asked his stepdaughters what they would like for a present.

'Oh,' said the eldest daughter, 'bring me some beautiful gowns of silk, I am sick of my old dresses.'

Yes, that is what she said although her gowns were almost brand new.

The second sister looked at herself in the mirror and stroked her white throat.

'Bring me a pearl necklace,' she said, 'to wear around my beautiful throat.'

Yes, she said that, although she had enough jewels to make a king's ransom.

Then the father looked at Cinderella. 'What about you?' he asked.

Cinderella glanced up from where she was scrubbing the floor.

'Father,' she said, 'bring me the first branch which brushes your hat on the way home.'

The father went to the fair and bought dresses of fine silk, and a pearl necklace. On his way, as he rode through a thicket, a hazel twig brushed against his hat and he remembered Cinderella's request. When he got home he gave the gowns and pearls to his stepdaughters and the hazel twig to Cinderella. The sisters ran to their bedroom and dressed up, preening themselves before the mirror and saying how beautiful they were. But Cinderella went to her mother's grave and planted the hazel twig there and watered it with her tears.

Joy can come from sorrow, and the twig grew into a fine tree. Every day Cinderella went and sat under its leaves and, after a while, a little white bird began to perch in the tree and sing to the girl.

Now in the spring it happened that the King of the country had ruled for fifty years and he ordered that for three days there should be a carnival. He ordered that every girl in the Kingdom should come to a ball in his palace for the three nights so that his son, the Prince, could choose a bride.

When the two sisters heard this they were beside themselves with excitement. 'A ball!' they squeaked. 'A ball at the palace!' They dragged Cinderella from the scullery and made her polish their shoes and iron their gowns. 'And do it properly,' they hissed. 'The Prince will choose one of us for his bride.' And they tweaked Cinderella's nose and pulled her ears so that she would not forget.

Cinderella did as she was told but she, too, wanted to go to the ball. She asked her stepmother if she might go, and the stepmother stared at her as if she had gone mad.

'You go to the King's ball?' she screeched. 'You? Why, just take a look at yourself. You are dirty and ragged, and how could you dance in those clogs?' She screamed with laughter and slapped Cinderella's face for good measure. But Cinderella said that the King had given orders that every girl in the Kingdom should go to his ball.

'Very well,' snapped the stepmother. 'Go to the ball. But first—' she picked up a basket of peas, marched into the garden, and threw them on to the dust-heap. 'There,' she said. 'If you can pick up all the peas in half an hour and separate the good ones from the bad, then you can go.'

As the stepmother went into the house to snigger and giggle with her daughters, Cinderella kneeled down and began to pick up the peas. But the peas were so tiny that in half-an-hour she had scarcely picked up two handfuls.

'I shall never do this,' she said. 'And I shall not go to the King's ball.' But just then she heard a rustle of wings. She looked up, and there, perching on the clothes line, she saw the little white bird from the hazel tree which grew on her mother's grave.

The bird whistled a little song and then it said, 'Ask for help, Cinderella. Ask the birds of the air for help.'

Cinderella opened her arms and looked at the Heavens. 'Help me,' she called. 'Help me, you tame pigeons and you turtle doves. Help me, all you birds of the air.'

Immediately two grey pigeons fluttered down, and then turtle doves, and then sparrows and starlings and finches. All the birds of the air swarmed into the garden. The pigeons began to peck at the ashes, 'pick, pick, pick—' and all the other birds did the same; 'pick, pick, pick—' picking up the peas and putting the good ones in the basket and the bad ones in the dust-bin, and before one hour had passed all the peas had been gathered and sorted. Then the birds flew away.

Cinderella took the peas to her stepmother who scowled when she saw them. The sisters scowled, too, and they cried out, 'You cannot come in those rags. You would disgrace us. If you can find the proper clothes you can come.' Then, believing that Cinderella could never find fine clothes, they turned their proud, vain backs on her and hurried away to the palace.

Cinderella sat on a three-legged stool and sobbed, but as she sobbed she heard a tapping at the window and there was the white bird. It fluttered its wings and arched its neck, as if to say 'follow me', then it flew away.

Cinderella followed the bird to the graveyard where it settled in the hazel tree. Cinderella knelt under the tree and said:

> 'Rustle your leaves, hazel tree,
> Silver and gold throw over me.'

The branches of the tree waved and the leaves rustled as if a wind was blowing, except that there was no wind, and it was as if the tree was whispering a secret, except that there were no words spoken. Then, from the green shadows of the tree, the white bird threw down a dress of gold and silver, and slippers of silver and gold.

Cinderella ran home and changed into her new clothes and went to the ball. Her stepmother and stepsisters were there, parading like three peacocks, but they did not recognize the charming girl in the splendid dress as Cinderella. When they saw Cinderella it was only as a poor drudge covered in ashes, and it was beyond their wit to recognize her now.

But Cinderella was the most beautiful girl at the ball. The Prince danced with her the whole night through and would not allow anyone else to take her hand. When the ball ended at midnight he ordered his carriage and took Cinderella home. But when they arrived Cinderella slipped from the carriage, ran into the garden, and hid in the pigeon loft.

The Prince waited in the street until Cinderella's father returned home and told him that the unknown girl was hiding in the pigeon loft.

'Who can that be?' the father said. 'Surely it isn't Cinderella?'

He sent for a servant who hacked his way into the loft but there was no girl there. Then they went into the house and found Cinderella, sleeping in the ashes and dressed in her old grey gown, for she had run to the graveyard and thrown down her dress and slippers and the white bird had taken them.

The Prince took one glance at Cinderella and shook his head. 'That's not her,' he said, and went back to the palace.

The next night there was another ball and when her parents and sisters had gone to the palace, Cinderella went to her mother's grave, knelt under the hazel tree, and said:

> 'Rustle your leaves, hazel tree,
> Silver and gold throw over me.'

Again the branches waved and the leaves rustled, although there was no wind, and the white bird threw down a dress of gold and pearls, and slippers of pearls and gold.

Cinderella changed into the dress and slippers and went to the ball. The guests were astonished at her beauty and her charm and her grace, and again the Prince danced with her the whole night through. But when the ball ended he did not take Cinderella home, instead he followed her at a distance.

'She will not escape from me this time,' he said. 'I will find out who she is and marry her.'

He followed Cinderella through the crooked streets of the town but when she reached her home Cinderella ran into the garden and hid in a pear tree. The Prince searched the garden. After a while, when Cinderella's father came home, the Prince told him that the fairest girl in the land was hiding in the pear tree.

'Well,' said the father, 'I don't know who that can be. The only girl in the house is Cinderella, and she certainly isn't the fairest girl in the land.'

However, he told his servant to bring an axe and chop the tree down, but there was no one in the branches, for Cinderella had run from the garden, given her clothes back to the bird, and was lying in the ashes.

The next night was the last night of the carnival and the last night of the ball. Cinderella went to her mother's grave and the little white bird threw down a dress of gold and diamonds and slippers of glass. At the ball Cinderella was so beautiful and full of grace that the other guests rubbed their eyes in wonder. 'Who can she be?' they asked. 'Who?' But not one person there recognized her.

All through the ball the Prince danced with Cinderella, but although he begged and pleaded with her she would not tell him her name and when the ball ended she slipped away and ran home.

But this time the Prince was ready. He had ordered his servants to smear pitch on the staircase and as Cinderella ran down the stairs her left slipper was stuck in the pitch and she had to leave it behind.

The Prince picked up the slipper and took it to his father, the King. 'Whoever this slipper fits must be my wife,' he said.

'Very well,' said the King. 'But how will you find the girl it belongs to?'

'That's all right,' said the Prince. 'When the girl ran away she left her footprints in black pitch all down the road.'

The next morning the Prince took his soldiers and followed the black footprints through the streets until he came to Cinderella's house. When the stepmother saw the Prince, and heard why he had come, she almost fainted, but she soon gathered her wits about herself.

'Oh, your Royal Highness,' she squeaked. 'Here are my beautiful daughters. They were both at the ball last night and they both lost their left slipper, the silly girls!'

The Prince thought it was odd that both the girls should have lost their left slipper but he was too polite to say so.

Instead he handed over the slipper and the mother bustled the elder daughter into the bedroom. The daughter peered at the slipper.

'This isn't mine, Mother,' she said.

The mother rolled her eyes at the ceiling. 'Don't be a fool,' she snapped. 'Put it on. Put it on and the Prince will marry you.'

The daughter tried the slipper but her feet were so big that she could not even get her big toe into it.

'Never mind,' said her mother. 'Here—' she took out a pair of scissors. 'I will cut your toe off.'

The daughter went white when she heard that and she began to cry but her mother would not be stopped.

'What is a toe?' she said. 'When you are Queen you won't need to walk, you will ride everywhere in a silver coach,' and she snipped the toe off.

The daughter choked back her scream, forced the slipper over her foot, and went out to the Prince. He placed her in his silver coach and they drove away to the palace to be married. However, their way took them past the grave of Cinderella's mother where the white bird sat in the hazel tree. As the coach rumbled past the bird sang:

> 'Turn and look, turn and look,
> There is blood inside the shoe.
> The slipper is too small, too small,
> And she is not the bride for you.'

The Prince looked down and saw that blood was dripping from the slipper the elder daughter was wearing. Through the glass he saw that her big toe had been cut off.

'Why, you cheat,' he said, and pushed her out of the coach. He held the slipper and told the coachman to drive back to Cinderella's house.

The mother bit her lip when she saw the Prince return but she was cunning.

'That elder daughter of mine is a terrible fraud,' she said. 'I am glad that you found her out. The slipper really belongs to my younger daughter.'

She pushed the younger daughter into the bedroom. This time the slipper went over the foot but the younger daughter could not get her heel into it.

'Never mind,' said her mother. 'What is a heel, anyway. When you are Queen you will never need to walk,' and she took a knife and hacked her daughter's heel off. 'There,' she panted. 'Now put the slipper on.'

The daughter put the slipper on and went to the Prince and he took her in his coach to the palace to be married. But again the coach went past the graveyard and again the white bird sang its song:

> 'Turn and look, turn and look,
> There is blood inside the shoe.
> The slipper is too small, too small,
> And she is not the bride for you.'

The Prince looked and saw blood staining the younger daughter's white satin stocking. 'Another cheat,' he cried, and kicked her off the coach.

He went to Cinderella's house and burst in. 'Now,' he said, and he was very angry, 'now I want to see the person this slipper truly belongs to. Where is she?'

The father shrugged. 'There is no one else here it could possibly belong to,' he said.

'Yet,' said the Prince, 'the footprints led here. Have you no other daughter?'

'Well, I do have one,' said the father. 'But she is only a dirty scrap of a thing my first wife left me. It couldn't possibly be her. All she does is sit in the ashes and weep.'

'Never mind that,' said the Prince. 'Bring her to me.'

The mother scowled. 'We couldn't possibly do that, she is too dirty.'

'Well wash her,' ordered the Prince. 'And hurry up about it.'

An order is an order, especially if it comes from a prince who can have your head chopped off if he feels like it, and so Cinderella was washed and brushed and brought into the sitting-room. There the Prince gave her the slipper and it fitted her like a second skin. Then she stood up and the Prince recognized her as the girl he had danced with.

'This is my true bride,' he said, 'and I will marry her. And when I am King, she will be my Queen.'

The stepmother and her two daughters burst into tears but the Prince pushed them out of the way and drove off with his bride; and as they passed the hazel tree the white bird sang:

> 'Turn and look, turn and look,
> There is no blood inside the shoe.
> The slipper is a perfect fit
> And she is the bride for you.'

Then two doves fluttered from the sky and landed on Cinderella's shoulders, one on her right shoulder and one on her left shoulder, and they cooed into her ears as the white bird flew overhead.

When the wedding took place in the cathedral, Cinderella's two stepsisters turned up! They hobbled down the aisle and elbowed their way into the best seats and sat there, grinning and waving at Cinderella as if she was their dearest friend! And when the Archbishop said that the Prince and his bride were man and wife and the Prince kissed Cinderella, the two sisters dabbed their eyes with their handkerchiefs as if they were crying with joy, although their tears were of bitter envy and rage.

The church bells rang and the organ played and the Prince led his wife out into the town. The sisters pushed their way out, too. But as they left two doves came down. One perched on the left shoulder of the elder daughter and one on the right shoulder of the younger daughter, and they each pecked an eye out. Then they changed places and pecked out the other eye so that, for their wickedness and cruelty and vanity and lying the two sisters were punished with blindness all the days of their lives.

Hansel and Gretel

I n olden times, a woodcutter and his wife lived by the edge of a vast forest. They had two children: a son called Hansel, and a daughter called Gretel.

The woodcutter was a poor man and there was never much food in the house. If the children asked what there was for their dinner they would often be told, 'Three jumps at the cupboard door and the first one there gets the knob,' and if they had bacon once a month then they were lucky. But one terrible year there was a famine, so severe that even the rats died of hunger.

The woodcutter and his wife scraped together what food they could, but there came a day when all that was left in the house were a few scraps of bread. That night, as they lay in bed, the wife turned to her husband.

'Listen,' she said. 'I have been thinking. We must get rid of our children.'

The woodcutter thought that he was having a nightmare. 'Get rid of our children?' he cried. 'What are you saying?'

'I am saying this,' his wife said. 'If we keep them then we might as well start digging our graves now because

214

we will all die of hunger. If we get rid of the children then at least you and I will survive. Tomorrow we will take Hansel and Gretel into the forest and leave them there.'

The woodcutter moaned. 'But the wolves will kill them and eat them.'

'I know,' the wife said. 'At least that will be a quick death.'

The woodcutter felt as if his heart would burst, but he agreed, although he groaned with sorrow.

'Shut up, you fool,' snapped his wife. 'Do you want the children to hear?'

But she was too late. The children had heard. They were so hungry that they could not sleep and their sharp ears had listened to every word.

Gretel began to cry. 'Ah,' she sobbed. 'Tomorrow we will be left in the forest and the wolves will eat us.'

Hansel put his arms around Gretel. 'Don't cry, little one,' he comforted her. 'The wolves will not have us.'

He slipped from the bedroom, tiptoed down the stairs, and went outside. The moon was shining and the pebbles around the house glittered as brightly as new pennies. Hansel filled his pockets with pebbles and then went back into the house.

'Don't worry, Gretel,' he said. 'Tomorrow night we will sleep in our own little beds.'

The morning came and as the sun rose the mother roused the children.

'Come now,' she said. 'We are going into the forest to search for food.'

The children got up, washed and dressed, and their mother gave them each a tiny scrap of bread.

'Take this,' she said, 'but don't eat it until midday.'

As the birds began to sing the woodcutter swung his

axe over his shoulder and led the way into the forest, and he had a miserable face, you can be sure.

They trudged on but Hansel lagged behind. Every now and then, he dropped a pebble, and he kept glancing over his shoulder to make sure that he could see them. After a little while the mother noticed that Hansel was peering behind.

'What are you looking at?' she asked.

Hansel pointed to the cottage. 'I was just looking at our little cat sitting on the roof. Look, it is waving goodbye.'

'Don't be stupid,' the mother said. 'That is the chimney pot,' and she tweaked Hansel's ear and pushed him forward.

On and on the family walked, twisting and turning through thickets and tangled brushes, but all the time Hansel dropped his pebbles behind him.

At last the woodcutter halted. 'Now, children,' he said. 'Your mother and I are going to look for food. You stay here and rest and I will make a fire so that you are warm while we are away.'

He made a fire and when it was burning well the mother said, 'Now stay here until we come to take you home.'

The mother and father went off into the forest and Hansel and Gretel sat by the fire. At midday they ate their scrap of bread, then Hansel told Gretel the story of Tom Thumb, and still the father and mother did not return.

The night came. In the darkness the trees creaked and wolves bayed. Gretel began to cry but Hansel patted her on the head.

'It's all right,' he said. 'As soon as the moon shines we will go home.'

The moon rose and gazed down on the world and in its silvery light the pebbles Hansel had dropped shone like fireflies and led Hansel and Gretel all the way through the forest to their home.

When the two children walked into the cottage the father was overjoyed and the mother pretended to be, but she scolded them, saying, 'You naughty children. We came for you but you had left the fire after we had told you to stay there. Now go to bed at once.'

A few days later the wife looked into the cupboard. There was a little bread and a lot of dust, and that was all. She shook her head and that night she again told her husband that they would have to get rid of the children.

The father struck his clenched fist on the table. 'No!' he shouted. 'No! It is better that we share our last morsel with them.'

'You fool,' said the wife. 'Is it better that four die, or two? Anyway, you agreed before, so you can agree now.'

Well, he who says A must say B, and he who consents the first time finds that he must consent the second time and so, although he was almost out of his mind with grief, the father agreed.

But once again the children were awake and heard their parents. Hansel slipped out of bed to collect more pebbles but his mother had locked the door.

Gretel began to cry but Hansel took her hand.

'Now, sister,' he said. 'Don't distress yourself. Sleep in peace. God will not forsake us.'

Early the next morning the mother dragged the children from their beds and when they had washed and dressed she gave them a piece of bread each and the family set out into the forest. On the way Hansel lagged behind again, breaking his bread, spreading the crumbs on the path, and, every now and then, looking over his shoulder to make sure that he could see them.

The mother noticed this and asked what he was doing.

'Oh,' said Hansel, 'I am just looking at my little pet dove. It is on the roof of the cottage, waving goodbye to me.'

'Don't talk rubbish,' said the mother. 'That is the sun shining on the chimney pot.' And she pulled Hansel's hair.

The family walked on into the forest, deeper and further than any man had ever gone before, into forest so deep and tangled that the sun could not shine through the wild branches of the trees. At length they stopped and the woodcutter made a fire.

'Stay here, children,' he said. 'We will go and find food but we will return before nightfall.'

The children sat by the fire all day but when night came the parents had not come back. Gretel was afraid but Hansel smiled at her.

'Rest your soul,' he said. 'I have left a trail of crumbs behind us. As soon as the moon rises we will follow the crumbs all the way home.'

As the owls began to call, the moon looked over the edge of the world and Hansel and Gretel set out to walk home.

'Watch for the crumbs, Gretel,' said Hansel, but although they looked as hard as they could there were no crumbs to be found because the birds of the forest had eaten them all!

Without the crumbs the children could not find their way out of the forest and they spent the night huddled together in the branches of a tree, whimpering at every strange sound—and the forest was full of them.

When day came they wandered through the forest, turning this way and that, sloshing through bogs and being scratched and gashed by thorns. They called for help but, deep in the heart of the wild forest there was no one to hear them, only the wild animals which ran away as the children blundered near them. Now and again they found berries, but the fruit was green and bitter and made their stomachs ache. Ah! As they wandered they cried because their father and mother had deserted them. They were the saddest children who ever strayed across the face of the earth.

Night came and they slept in a tree, and when the dawn broke it was the third day since they had left their cottage. If we do not find food today, thought Hansel, then we will surely die of hunger.

Once more they stumbled through the forest and then, at noon, as they rested near a stream, they saw a tree with golden leaves, and on the tree was a bird with wings of silver. The bird sang so beautifully that Hansel and Gretel forgot their hunger. But after a little while the bird stopped singing and soared around their heads as if to say, 'Follow me. Follow me.'

The bird flew away and the children followed it. Soon they came to a path and the path led to a glade, and in the glade was a house. Hansel and Gretel skipped for joy when they saw the house. They ran towards it and found that its walls were made of wheaten bread! And the roof was gingerbread and the windows were clear sugar!

'Oh,' cried Hansel, and his eyes were as big and round as an owl's. 'Now we are saved, Gretel. Come, I will have some of the roof and you take a piece of window. That will be nice and sweet.'

The children sat down to enjoy their food but as they were eating they heard a voice, and the voice sang:

> 'Nibble, nibble,
> Nibble, gnaw,
> Who is nibbling
> My little house?'

The children did not answer, and the voice called again:

> 'Tip, tap, tip,
> Who rattles my door?'

Hansel wiped his mouth and called back:

> 'The wind, the wind, the blessed wind,
> It is the wind which blows from heaven.'

He crammed some gingerbread into his mouth but as he did so the door opened and an old woman hobbled out. She was a dear old woman. Her eyes were bright blue and twinkled like two stars, and her cheeks were as ruddy as autumn apples. She looked at Hansel and Gretel and shook her head:

'Goodness gracious me,' she said. 'You poor little things. What a state you are in!'

And Hansel and Gretel were in a state; scratched and muddy and with berry stains all over their faces. They were ready to burst into tears, but the old woman smiled at them.

'You must have got lost in the forest,' she said. 'But don't be afraid, you are safe now. Come into my little house and I will look after you.'

She took them into her house, washed their faces, then cooked them pancakes with sugar and gave them apples and nuts. When they had eaten she tucked them up in two beds with fine white sheets, so that Hansel and Gretel thought that they were in Heaven. They said their prayers together and then the old woman kissed them goodnight and left them to sleep.

But as the children slept the old woman crept back into their bedroom with a candle, and by the flickering light of the candle she stared down on Hansel and Gretel, and her eyes were not bright blue, like two stars, but red, like the eyes of a merciless wolf, and her cheeks were not full and ruddy, like two autumn apples, but haggard and withered, like a rotten turnip. The woman stared down on the two sleeping innocents and then stole to her own room.

There she sat in a rocking chair and rocked to and fro, rubbing her skinny hands together and smacking her gums. She rocked to and fro and laughed, 'Hee, hee, hee; hee, hee, hee!' For the woman was a witch, and a wicked, evil one whose heart was as black as midnight. And she had built her house to entice children. Then, when she had caught them she killed them and cooked them and ate them! Witches have red eyes and cannot see very far but, like wild beasts, they have a fine sense of smell and they can scent when children draw near them, and that is how the witch knew that Hansel and Gretel were lost in the forest and that is why she had changed herself into a silver bird to draw them near. But the witch lived so deep in the forest that not many children came her way and so this was a real feast day for her.

All night the witch rocked in her rocking-chair, but as the first cock crowed for the first time she leaped to her feet and went into the bedroom and looked down on the children and smacked her lips. Then she seized Hansel and, before he had time to wake, she had dragged him from his bed and rushed him across the yard and locked him in a little stall with a barred door.

The witch cackled with joy and then she shook Gretel awake. 'Get up,' she spat. 'Get up, lazy-bones. Bring water and make the fire and cook the best food in the house. Your brother is just skin and bone, but I will fatten him, that I will. And when he is fat enough I will cook him and eat him!'

Gretel screamed and cried but it was no use. She had to do as the witch said. She cooked chicken and pie and the witch made Hansel eat it, although all that Gretel got was the chicken's bones.

The next morning the witch went to the stall. 'Hansel,' she commanded, 'poke your finger through the bars so that I can feel how fat you are getting.'

But Hansel was a clever lad, indeed he was. Instead of poking his finger through the bars he stuck out the chicken's claw.

The witch felt it. 'Aieeh!' she wailed. 'You are too skinny to put in the pot. But you will be fat, you will be.'

Every day Gretel cooked the finest food: chops and steak and trout, and every day Hansel ate it, and every day the witch went to the stall, and every day Hansel poked the chicken's claw through the bars for the witch to feel.

This went on for four weeks, and then the witch said that she would wait no longer.

'Gretel,' she said, 'your brother will not fatten up, but fat or thin I am going to eat him today.'

Gretel had to bring the water and pour it in the cauldron although her tears flowed so much that she could have filled the pan with those alone. 'Dear God,' she cried. 'We would have been better off in the forest with the wild beasts. At least we would have died together. Oh, Lord, deliver us from this evil.'

The witch cracked Gretel on the head with the ladle. 'None of that,' she croaked. 'None of your whining prayers in this house. Now get in the oven and see if the pastry for my Hansel-pie is baked nice and brown. My eyes are so weak that I cannot see properly.'

Gretel peeked into the red-hot oven but, just as Hansel was a clever lad, so she was a clever girl. She knew that the witch wanted to push her into the oven and bake her.

'I can't get my head in,' she said. 'The opening is too small.'

'You stupid creature,' snarled the witch. 'You good-for-nothing. I will show you.'

She hobbled to the oven and bent down and poked her head into the door. 'Look,' she said. 'This is how you—'

But she never finished her sentence because Gretel seized her scraggy neck and shoved *her* into the oven and slammed the door on her. Then it was the witch's turn to scream and howl! She hammered on the great iron door of the oven but she could not break out and so she was burned to ashes and bone.

Gretel ran to Hansel and unlocked the cage. Her brother jumped out like a bird which has been freed.

'The witch is dead, Hansel,' cried Gretel. 'The witch is dead!'

How the two children skipped and leaped for joy!

'The witch is dead,' they sang. 'The witch is dead!' And the animals in the thickets heard them and bleated and barked with joy, too, for the evil of the witch had poisoned and infected the whole forest.

The children went into the house and, in the drawers and cupboards, they found pearls and diamonds which the wicked old woman had stolen from the people she had beguiled to her and murdered. Gretel filled her apron full of diamonds and Hansel stuffed his pockets full of pearls.

'These are better than pebbles or breadcrumbs,' Hansel said. 'But now we must be off. We still have to find our way out of this enchanted forest.'

Hand in hand they set off, but the forest was as mysterious as ever and soon they were lost. Nevertheless, they walked on and after two hours they came to a river, broad and deep.

'Oh dear,' said Hansel. 'How can we cross over this river? There is not a boat in sight,' and for the first time he, too, began to cry.

'Now now,' Gretel said. 'Cheer up. Where there is a will there is a way. Look, there is a white duck. I will ask her for help.' And she sang:

> 'Little duck, little duck,
> On this river deep and wide,
> Two little children ask you, dear,
> Take us to the other side.'

The duck bobbed her head, paddled to the bank, and looked at them through its gentle, brown eyes. 'Quack, quack,' it cried. 'Quack, quack,' and opened its wings to make a seat. Hansel jumped on and told Gretel to sit behind him, but she shook her head.

'That would be too much for the little duck,' she said. 'You go first and I will follow.'

The duck quacked with pleasure at Gretel's kind words and took Hansel across the river and then she carried

Gretel over safely. Hansel gave the duck some gingerbread from the witch's cottage and she swam away quacking happily, 'The witch is dead! The witch is dead!'

Once they had crossed the river Hansel and Gretel found themselves in open fields. Soon they came to a path they knew and before very long they saw their own cottage nestling against the forest's edge. The little cat ran out to meet them, and the little dove flew out to greet them. Hansel held the cat and Gretel held the dove and they burst into the cottage where their father gave a great shout of joy when he saw them. Poor man, his wife had died, and since the children had been left in the forest he had not had a moment's peace or joy. But Gretel spilled diamonds from her apron, and Hansel threw down pearls from his pocket, until the whole house glittered and gleamed with light. So all their sorrows were over and, lovingly, they lived together till the end of their days.

And so the tale is done, but look! There is a mouse! Whoever catches her can make a great hat from her fur!

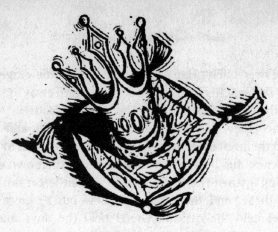

Snow White and the
Seven Dwarfs

One day in the silence of midwinter, long ago, a Queen sat by her window, sewing. Snowflakes drifted past the window which had a frame of ebony, a wood as black as night. As the Queen dreamily watched the snowflakes spinning down she accidentally pricked her finger with her needle and three bright drops of blood splashed on to the cloth she was embroidering.

The Queen looked at the blood, and the ebony window frame, and the snow. If I ever have a daughter, she thought, I would like her to be as red as blood, as black as the ebony window-frame, and as white as the snow.

A year or so passed and the Queen did have a daughter and her wish came true, for the baby had lips as red as blood, hair as black as ebony, and skin as white as snow. The Queen remembered the day in midwinter when she had pricked her finger and so she called the child Snow White.

Sadly the Queen died and after a year had passed the King married again. Now the new Queen was beautiful, and she was proud of her beauty. She could not bear to think that there might be any other woman in the land who was as beautiful, and she had a way of finding out if there was one.

In a dark tower in the palace the Queen had a secret room, and in the room she had a mirror. But it was no ordinary mirror, as you will find out

Every day the Queen went up the spiral stairs of the dark tower and entered her secret room and stared into the mirror, and the mirror stared back. But there was no reflection in its glass, only a pale, milky-blue haze like a blind man's eye. Queen and mirror would stare at each other and then the Queen would say:

> '*Spieglein, Spieglein, an der Wand,*
> *Wer ist die schönste Frau in dem ganzen Land?*'

Which means in English:

> 'Mirror, mirror, on the wall,
> Who is the most beautiful woman in all the
> land?'

Then the mirror would ripple, like a pool when a stone has been thrown into it, and strange shapes and images shimmered in the milky-blue haze, for the mirror was searching every hill and dale, and every town and village in the kingdom. And then it would speak! In a whisper the mirror would say:

> '*Ihr, Frau Königin seid die schönste Frau im*
> *Land.*'

Which means:

'You, Lady Queen, are still the most beautiful
   woman in the land.'

Then the Queen would be satisfied. She would smile
and rub her hands together, lock the door of her secret
room, and go down the spiral stairs.

Five years passed, and another five, but one day when
the Queen went to her secret room and stared into the
mirror and the mirror stared blindly back as the Queen
asked:

   Spieglein, Spieglein, an der Wand,
   Wer ist die schönste Frau in dem ganzen Land?'

the mirror rippled and whispered, only this time it
said:

   'Frau Königin, Ihr seid die schönste hier,
   Aber Schneewittchen ist noch tausendmal schöner
   als Ihr.

Which means:

'Lady Queen, you are the most beautiful
   woman here,
But Snow White is a thousand times more
   beautiful than you!'

When the Queen heard the mirror her heart almost
burst with envy and hatred. 'I cannot bear it,' she cried. 'I
cannot bear it,' and she was without pity or mercy.

She left her secret room and sent for her huntsman. 'Now,' she said. 'You must take Snow White into the forest. Take her far away where the mountains rise and kill her.'

'Kill her?' said the huntsman. 'Kill Snow White?'

'Yes.' The Queen hissed like a venomous snake. 'And to prove that you have killed her, bring me her heart and her lungs and her liver and I will cook them with salt and eat them.'

The huntsman could not believe his ears, but the Queen said that if he did not do as she commanded then she would poison him, so the next morning he took Snow White and led her into the forest, saying that he would show her the secret places where the fawns played.

All day the huntsman led Snow White deep into the forest until, at evening, he came to where the mountains rose. There he drew out his hunting knife and held it over Snow White but he could not bring himself to strike her.

Ah, he thought, how can I slaughter an innocent child? No, I cannot bring myself to do it.

He put his knife in its sheath. I know what I will do, he thought. I will leave her here in the forest. She will never find her way back to the palace and the wild animals will kill her.

And so he left Snow White in the wilderness. But as he was riding back to the palace he killed a young deer and took out its heart and liver and lungs. 'These are like a child's,' he said. 'The Queen will never know the difference.'

He was right. The Queen took the heart and the lungs and the liver, cooked them with salt, and ate them.

As the Queen was eating, Snow White was alone in the forest. For a long time she called for the huntsman but the only answer was the whistling of the birds. She heard a bear growl, and she heard a wolf howl, and she was so frightened that she ran through the forest. The thorns slashed her and the sharp stones cut her poor feet and every time she stopped to rest she heard wolves and bears and ran on again. But even the wild beasts had pity on her and although, through the leaves, they spied on her with their bright eyes, not one of them tried to catch her and eat her.

All afternoon Snow White ran through the forest and then, as night brought darkness across the land, she came to a glade, and at the end of the glade was a cottage, but it was not an ordinary cottage. No, it was small. In fact it was so tiny that Snow White had to kneel down to knock on the door!

Snow White rapped the knocker but there was no answer. She rapped again but the only sound inside the cottage was the ticking of a clock.

Ah, thought Snow White. There is nobody at home, but surely whoever owns this cottage would not grudge a poor child shelter, and she opened the door and crept in.

The last rays of the sun shone through the window and by its light Snow White could see what was inside the cottage. Everything was tiny, but neat and clean. There was a little table and on a spotless table-cloth there were seven plates and seven spoons and seven cups, no bigger than acorns, and by every place there was a chair like an infant's. Lined up in a row against the wall were seven little beds, each with a snowy counterpane and the whole cottage shone and sparkled as if everything in it was made of silver and gold.

In each little plate there was some broth. But although Snow White was very hungry she only took a small spoonful from each helping because she did not want to seem greedy. When she had eaten, Snow White was so tired that she had to sleep. She tried every bed, but one was too small, another was too hard, the next was too soft; the seventh bed, however, was just right and in that one she curled up and went fast asleep.

Night came and from the mountains there came the sound of footsteps:

Tramp, tramp, tramp.
Tramp, tramp, tramp, tramp.

The sound of seven men marching, the seven men who owned the cottage where Snow White lay sleeping. But they were not ordinary men. They were seven dwarfs. Seven tiny, gnarled men with long beards who spent their days in their mine under the mountains where they dug for rubies and emeralds. Each of the dwarfs had a lantern and when they entered their cottage they saw at once that someone had been in their house.

'Aiee!' said the first dwarf. 'Who has been sitting on my chair?'

'And who has been eating off my plate?' asked the second dwarf.

The third said, 'Who has eaten my broth?'

'And who has been at my bread?' said the fourth.

The fifth pulled a face, 'Someone has used my spoon.'

'And someone has used my knife,' said the sixth.

'Yes, and my fork,' said the seventh.

The dwarfs looked at each other and were afraid, because they were only tiny, you know. Then one held up his lantern.

'Look,' he said. 'Someone has been in my bed!'

Each dwarf ran to his bed and saw that it had been disturbed. They were cross and frightened, but then the seventh dwarf cried out.

'Ah!' he called. 'See here.'

The other dwarfs ran to him and held up their lanterns and stared down on Snow White who was sound asleep.

'My God, my God,' the dwarfs whispered. 'What a beautiful child,' and they looked at her with wonder and amazement. 'Who can she be?' they whispered. 'Where can she have come from?'

So touched were the dwarfs by Snow White's innocent sleep that they did not waken her but each tiptoed off to his own bed, all except the seventh dwarf because Snow White was in his bed. He slept with the other dwarfs, an hour with each of them.

The dwarfs woke up early the next morning and sat in a circle around Snow White, waiting for her to wake up, too. The child slept late but at last she sighed a little and opened her eyes, and saw the seven tiny, gnarled men staring at her.

Snow White gave a little scream, but the dwarfs smiled and nodded so that she lost her fear and smiled back at them. The dwarfs made her some breakfast and when she had eaten they sat with her by the fire, each on his own little stool, and with Snow White sitting on the bed.

The dwarfs asked Snow White where she had come from, and she told them how the huntsman had brought her into the forest but had left her to the wild beasts instead of killing her, and how she had wandered through the forest until, at last, she found their cottage.

The dwarfs lit their pipes and smoked as Snow White told her tale. When she had finished they looked grave and shook their heads for they could hardly credit that a mother should behave so to her own child, or, indeed, that anyone could be so cruel.

Finally the eldest dwarf spoke.

'Snow White,' he said, 'this is a terrible story, terrible. I have never heard of anything so terrible. But whatever happens, you must not go back to the palace otherwise your mother will certainly kill you, one way or the other. No, that will never do. But what I suggest is this: nobody knows that you are here in our little cottage and so you are safe. Now then, if you would like to be our housekeeper we will be very glad to have you. Would you like to stay with us?'

Snow White looked at the kindly faces of the dwarfs. 'Oh, yes,' she said.

'Good,' said the dwarf. 'Then when we are in our mine you can cook and wash and keep the house clean. But, Snow White, we must work under the mountain all day and you will be alone here. Whatever happens you must not let anyone in. Who knows, your mother might just find out where you are and want to do evil to you.'

Snow White agreed and the dwarfs went off to work and she kept the little cottage as bright and sparkling as a new pin.

As Snow White kept house for the dwarfs, far away across the forest, the Queen, her mother, could not rest. All night long she felt a gnawing anguish in her breast and, as the first cock crowed, she rose from her bed and hurried to her secret room and stared into her mirror and asked who was the fairest woman in the land. And the mirror rippled and whispered:

'Queen, you are the most beautiful in this
room,
But far away, by the mountains,
Cared for by the seven dwarfs,
Snow White is still a thousand times more
beautiful than you.'

The Queen struck her breast. 'No,' she spat. 'No, it
cannot be. Snow White is dead. I have eaten her heart and
her liver and her lungs. Mirror, you lie. Tell me that you
lie.' But the mirror whispered that it spoke only of what it
saw.

The Queen knew that the mirror only spoke the truth
and then she knew that the huntsman had deceived her
and that Snow White still lived. All night long the
Queen paced the corridors of the palace, for envy would
not let her rest. In the sickly grey light of dawn she
thought of a plan to rid herself of Snow White once and
for all.

The Queen painted her face so that she looked old and
wrinkled, and dressed herself in rags so that she looked
like an old pedlar. Disguised like this she went into the
forest until she came to the mountains and there, as the
mirror had told her, she found the house of the seven
dwarfs.

She knocked on the door of the cottage and called,
'Pretty things for sale. Pretty things for sale, cheap.'

Snow White peeped through the window and saw an
old woman holding up a tray full of pretty things, ribbons
and combs and rings. Why, she thought, it is only an old
pedlar woman. Surely she can do me no harm. And so,
forgetting the dwarf's warning, she opened the door and
pointed to a silken ribbon.

'How much is that?' she asked.

'Oh,' cackled the old woman. 'It is very cheap, but see how pretty it is. How charming it will look around your pretty neck. Let me put it on you.'

Snow White opened her collar and the old woman slipped the ribbon around her neck, but she twisted it and twisted it until Snow White choked and fell down as if dead.

'Ha!' cried the Queen. 'Now I am the fairest woman in the land,' and she ran back through the forest to the palace.

Not long after the Queen had gone it was evening. The dwarfs came back from their labour in the mines and were horrified to find their Snow White lying on the ground as if dead. They cut the ribbon away from her neck and poured cold water over her face and, little by little, the colour came back in Snow White's lips and she began to breathe again.

The dwarfs gave three cheers, but when they heard what had happened they frowned and shook their heads. The eldest dwarf shook his finger. 'That old pedlar woman was your wicked mother. Now you must remember our words and never speak to another stranger unless we are with you. Be sure that your mother will try to kill you again.'

Snow White thanked the dwarfs and promised that she would never let another stranger in the house. Then they all went to sleep.

While they slept the Queen reached the palace and ran to her secret room and asked the mirror who was now the most beautiful woman in the land. And the mirror rippled and whispered:

'Lady Queen, you are the fairest in this room,
  But far away, by the mountains,
  Cared for by the seven dwarfs,
  Snow White is still a thousand times more
  beautiful than you.'

'No,' cried the Queen. 'No, it is not true. It cannot be true.'

But the mirror whispered that it was so and the Queen knew that she had to believe it. That night the Queen went to the gallows and, with magic arts which she understood, she made a deadly poison and smeared it on a comb. Then she disguised herself as a poor woman and made her way to the cottage of the seven dwarfs. She knocked on the door and Snow White peeped through the window.

The Queen held up the comb. 'Will you buy this, my pretty one?' she asked.

Snow White shook her head. 'No,' she said. 'I must not let anyone in the house.'

'Ah,' sighed the Queen. 'See, I am an old widow. If I do not sell this pretty comb then I must go hungry tonight.'

Snow White felt sorry for the old widow. She opened the door and bought the comb.

'Now,' said the Queen. 'Let me show you how to pin the comb in your hair.' She dragged the comb through Snow White's hair, the poison worked, and Snow White fell to the ground in a deadly faint.

The Queen crooked her fingers like a claw. 'Now,' she cried, 'you model of beauty. Lie there and see what your beauty has brought you. Aye, none in the land shall equal me and *my* beauty.'

236

Then she wrapped her cloak around her and went through the forest alone, for she feared neither man nor beast.

Snow White lay on the ground and, as the poison of the comb ran through her veins, her limbs were as cold as ice and a deadly sweat beaded her forehead, and she was on the threshold of Death's kingdom. But, as the messenger of Death came for her soul, the seven dwarfs came tramping back from their mine and found her lying before the fire.

The eldest dwarf took Snow White by the hand and felt her pulse and then he ran his wise hand through her hair and found the poisoned comb. With one swift gesture he pulled the comb away and, at once, the deadly sweat left Snow White's forehead, she opened her eyes, and she breathed again the sweet air of the evening.

How the dwarfs shook their heads. They shook their heads and sighed. 'Little one,' they said—and they said it seven times over—'you must be careful.'

The youngest dwarf was cross. 'Why are you so foolish?' he said. But the eldest dwarf hushed him. 'Be quiet,' he growled. 'Our little Snow White is but a child. Do you expect to find old heads on young shoulders? No, no.' But all the same he said to Snow White, 'Now do be careful, my dear. We do not want to lose you.'

Then the dwarfs put a hot-water bottle in Snow White's bed, asked God to keep them from all harm, and went to sleep.

The moon wandered across the sky and the wind sighed in the pine trees and, as the world slept, the Queen went to her secret room, smiled at the mirror, and asked it if she was now the most beautiful woman in the land.

But her smile vanished as the mirror rippled and whispered:

> 'Lady Queen, you are the fairest in this room,
> But far away, by the mountains,
> Guarded by the seven dwarfs,
> Snow White is still a thousand times more
> beautiful than you!'

The Queen trembled as if a fever had seized her. She shook and trembled and the sweat beaded *her* forehead. But, as the clock struck twelve, she wiped her brow with a cold cloth, raised herself, and went down a deep staircase, down into the very depths of the castle, down and down, down dripping staircase after dripping staircase, past the dank dungeons and the poor skeletons of all those who had opposed her and her wicked ways, until she came to a place which no other eye but hers had ever seen; and there she took an apple from a cupboard and on it she breathed a spell so that the red cheek of the apple was full of a poison so deadly that even to look at it would make a person sick, but to touch it with one's lips was certain death. Then the Queen made herself up as a poor beggar woman and she put the apple in a basket and set off into the forest. But, as goodness has no end, wickedness does have an end. Just as the kindest action makes the angels sing for ever and for ever, so does the wickedest action exhaust itself, as a bee, by stinging, dies. As we shall see.

Dressed as an old beggar woman the Queen hobbled through the forest to the dwarfs' cottage. There she lay down before the door and moaned:

'Aiee, if there is anyone here, give me a drink of water for I am sick unto death.'

Snow White heard the cry and looked through the window. 'I am sorry,' she said, 'but I dare not give you water. I am forbidden to open the window.'

But as the child saw the old woman lying helpless before the door she felt pity. Surely, she thought, surely giving a glass of water cannot do harm.

The child opened the window and passed out a glass of water. The Queen drank and gave the glass back. 'Thank you,' she said. 'But one good turn deserves another. Here, take this apple.'

Snow White shook her head. 'No thank you,' she said.

The Queen smiled. 'You are wise,' she cried. 'But the apple is good—look.' She held up the apple and it was so red and wholesome looking that Snow White's mouth watered. But still she would not take it.

'I know,' said the Queen. 'You are afraid that it is poisoned. What a clever child you are, to be sure. But there is no reason to fear. See—' She took a knife and cut the apple in half. 'See? I will eat this half.' She bit at her piece of apple and swallowed it and Snow White could not resist any longer. She took the red half of the apple and put it in her mouth and swallowed. The poisoned slice of apple stuck in her throat and she fell down as one who is dead.

The Queen's eyes glittered and she laughed. 'Now,' she cried. 'Black as ebony, red as blood, white as snow! Dead you are and dead you will stay. This time the dwarfs cannot help you.'

Laughing and cackling the Queen fled to the palace and ran to her mirror. 'Now,' she breathed, 'answer me truthfully:

'Spieglein, Spieglein, an der Wand.
Wer ist die schönste Frau in dem ganzen Land?'

And the mirror whispered:

'Frau Königin, Ihr seid die schönste im Land:
Lady Queen, you are the most beautiful in
the land.'

Then, as far as a wicked and envious heart can rest, the Queen did.

In the evening the dwarfs came back from their mine and found Snow White lying on the floor. Everything they could do they did. They unlaced her dress and combed her hair and they washed her with wine and water. But they could not find anything poisonous and they could not cure the child.

'Ah,' they sobbed, 'she is dead. Our pretty one is truly dead.'

They laid Snow White out on the table and for three days they sat with her, weeping and sobbing. Then the time had come to bury her but she looked so sweet and beautiful that they could not bear to place her in the ground. From their mine they brought crystal and made a coffin and placed Snow White in it so that they could see her. Then on the coffin, in letters of gold, they wrote her name and wrote that she was the daughter of a king. They carried the coffin to a ledge on the mountainside and surrounded it with flowers, and one dwarf was always by it to keep it safe. Even the beasts mourned for Snow White, and the birds came and perched by the coffin; first an owl, then a raven, and then a dove.

Seven years passed and Snow White lay in her crystal

coffin as though she was not dead, but only in a long and dreamless sleep. Then, one day, a prince came hunting over the mountain. When he saw the coffin and Snow White lying inside it, he was so dazed by her beauty that he fell on his knees.

'Let me have this crystal coffin,' he said to the dwarfs. 'I will give you anything your hearts desire.'

The dwarfs shook their heads. 'No, no,' they said. 'We would not part with our dear Snow White for the world and all within it.'

The Prince stood up. 'Then let me have it as a gift,' he said, 'for I cannot live without seeing this beautiful Princess, and I will honour her and protect her all the days of my life.'

The dwarfs put their heads together and, out of pity for the Prince, they agreed to let him take the coffin and Snow White. The Prince called to his servants to carry the coffin to his palace, but as they lifted it, one of the servants stumbled on a stone and the coffin struck the ground, and the shock dislodged the poisoned apple from Snow White's throat. She opened her eyes and lifted the lid of the coffin.

'Where am I?' she asked. 'Is this a dream?'

The Prince leaned over her. 'No,' he said. 'It is not a dream. You have slept the sleep of death for seven years, but now you are well and have returned to this world.'

The dwarfs leaped for joy and the beasts bounded through the forest as they heard the news that Snow White was alive again. The Prince asked Snow White if she would be his bride. She asked the dwarfs and they agreed, and the Prince took Snow White and the seven dwarfs to his father's castle.

Before long the Prince married Snow White and his

father the King gave a great ball and invited all the other kings and queens. And one of the queens he invited was Snow White's mother.

The Queen dressed herself in all her finery, but before she left to go to the ball she went to her secret room and stood before the mirror and asked:

> 'Mirror, mirror, on the wall,
>   Who is the most beautiful in all the land?'

She smoothed her black tresses and held her head proudly as she waited for the mirror's answer for, with Snow White dead, she knew that she was the most beautiful woman in the world. But when she heard the mirror speak she raised her hand as if she would strike the whole world dead, for the mirror whispered:

> 'Lady Queen, you are the most beautiful here,
>   But the young Princess at the ball is a
>   thousand times
>   More beautiful than you!'

The Queen cursed and spat in her rage and she was so jealous that she said she would not go to the ball. But, just as she could not bear to go, so she could not bear to stay away, and in the end she went. She swept into the ballroom and when she saw that the young Princess was Snow White she was paralysed with rage and fear so that she could not move at all. But the old King said, 'You have come to dance, and dance you shall.'

His servants brought in a pair of white-hot iron clogs and the Queen was forced to put them on and she danced, then. Aye, she danced until she dropped dead.

242

And as the Queen dropped dead, in her secret room the mirror fell from the wall and shattered into a thousand fragments. If you can ever find your way into that secret room you will find the fragments still lying there and you will see that in every fragment there is a reflection, and every reflection is of Snow White, as beautiful as ever, surrounded by her children and the seven dwarfs.

But you will not hear the mirror whisper, for its voice has been stilled for ever.

The Old Man and
the Dog-Dish

A stonemason once lived on the plain of Holstein. He was a fine, strapping man who could swing his hammer the livelong day, and his chisel cut through the hardest stone as if it were cheese. But time, that thief, stole his strength away. He became old and weak, his wife died, and he had to go and live with his son and daughter-in-law.

They took him in but they had no love for him. As he sat at the table his hand shook so that his broth spilled from his spoon and ran on to his beard and his waistcoat and stained the table-cloth.

The couple were ashamed of the old man, and one day the daughter-in-law said that she was sick of the sight of him. From then on he had to sit in a dark corner behind the stove.

The old man's eyes, which had been as blue as cornflowers turned milky-grey and he could scarcely see the bowl he ate from. One day, as he sat in his dark corner, his hands trembled so much that his bowl slipped from his fingers and smashed on the floor.

'Ah!' cried the daughter-in-law. 'I knew that would happen. Look, my fine delft bowl broken. Well, you won't break another.' And she made the old man eat from an old wooden dog-dish.

The man and his wife had a son who was five years old. One day his mother and father found him cutting at a piece of wood.

'What are you making?' they asked.

The child looked up through his innocent eyes. 'Why, mother,' he smiled, 'why, father, I am making you a present. This is a wooden dish for you to eat from when you grow old, too.'

AND NOW we have seen some of the treasures the poor boy found in the chest buried in the snow on that winter's day so long ago. There are many more.

Author's Note

We are indebted for these famous fairy stories, or, as they are more properly known, house tales, to the brothers Jacob and Wilhelm Grimm of Germany.

In the course of studying the roots of mythology and language the brothers were told these tales by German peasants. They had not, before then, been written down. They were published for the first time, in three volumes, in 1812, 1815, and 1822, and have been reprinted, with some alterations, in many languages, and in many idioms, innumerable times.

Knowing this, the reader may be tempted to ask why a new edition is called for. I might answer by quoting John Ruskin's comment on folk-tales: 'They are like clouds which alter their shapes as they move across the sky but which retain, always, their same composition.' In other words I have translated freely, although I hope accurately, but in the language of our times; as Scripture says, 'The letter kills, but the spirit gives life.' I have tried to remain faithful to the spirit of the originals while, as the peasants who retold these tales did, telling them in the light of our own experience.

I have made my selection as varied as possible, including most of the old favourites, but printing some tales which are not, perhaps, as widely known as they deserve to be. If any reader feels that I should have chosen differently I can only say that these are merely thirty out of two hundred and ten stories and legends in the complete works.

For her assistance with the texts I should like to express my thanks to Mireille Gansel, Agrégée d'Allemand, Maître de Conférences, Université de Paris VIII.

PETER CARTER
St. Martial de Viveyrols
1980

Also in this series

Fairy Tales from Andersen
L.W. Kingsland
0 19 275010 0

The Ugly Duckling, Thumbelina, the Snow Queen, and the Little Mermaid are just some of the magical characters in Hans Christian Andersen's famous fairy tales. This collection has all the well-loved favourites, as well as some of Andersen's lesser known stories, and is bound to enchant new readers as much as it will please those who are already familiar with these classic stories.

One Thousand and One Arabian Nights
Geraldine McCaughrean
0 19 275013 5

'Woman's love is as long as the hairs on a chicken's egg!'

So says King Shahryar who kills a new wife every night, before she can stop loving him. But new bride Shahrazad has a clever plan to save herself. Her nightly stories—of Sinbad the Sailor, Ali Baba, and the Jinni of the Lamp— are so exciting that King Shahryar finds himself postponing her execution again and again . . .

This is a completely original version of the Arabian Nights by award-winning author, Geraldine McCaughrean.

'A brilliant tour de force'
                    Junior Bookshelf

Fairy Tales from England
James Reeves
0 19 275014 3

Giant-killing Johnny Gloke, a princess with a sheep's head, and a frog prince at the World's End are just some of the fairy-tale characters you'll find in this collection of stories, along with better-known tales such as Dick Whittington and Tom Thumb. Greedy giants, handsome princes, wicked queens, and a liberal sprinkling of magic all help to make sure this collection of traditional English fairy tales has something for everyone.

Fairy Tales from Scotland
Barbara Ker Wilson
0 19 275012 7

Gallant knights, the enchanting Elf Queen, witches, wizards, and wee faery folk . . . you'll find them all in this exciting collection of Scottish fairy tales and legends. Whether you prefer Highland legends, ancient sagas, or warrior adventures, there's something for everyone in this collection—along with a good helping of Gaelic magic!